I0538871

Chains of Blood

The Second of Severn

J. L. O'Rourke

Copyright 2015
Published by Millwheel Press Limited
(originally published 2013 as Daisy Chains)

ISBN 978-0-473-31768-3

Discover other titles by J. L. O'Rourke
Blood in the Wings: The First of Severn
Power Ride: An Avi Livingstone murder mystery

Acknowledgements:

While the majority of the characters in the Severn series are fictional inventions of my imagination and are not based on any real person, my thanks to the two real theatre crew who gave their permission to allow me to exaggerate their personalities and reinvent them into vampires. Those people know who they are – thank you. If anyone else thinks that they recognise themselves in a character – I guarantee that it is purely unintentional. Thank you, too, to my cover models, Skip and Tama.

Cover photo by Bethany Nehoff.

CHAPTER ONE

"Not again! I don't believe it!"

"I believe it. The guy's a moron!"

"Tell me something I don't know." I flicked a switch on the comms unit that was hooked, with a multitude of other gadgets, to the utility belt around my black jeans. "Okay, okay," I spoke into my headset microphone, interrupting the voice yammering at me through my headphones, "I know we've got no sound. That stupid little idiot has turned his pack off – again! Can you drag him off stage and turn him on or do I need to come down – 'cos if I do I'm going to beat the crap out of him then stuff the ..." I bit my tongue and left the sentence unfinished. Pulling my black beanie tighter under my headphones, I flicked off my microphone and grimaced at the man beside me. He grinned back and pointed across the expanse of lush green lawn to the makeshift stage on which a boy in green tights and a brown jerkin was singing soundlessly.

"I think they got the message," he laughed as a large woman, also clad totally in black, stormed angrily across the stage, grabbed the boy by his shoulders, spun him around, lifted his jerkin, fumbled with something on the back of his tights, spun him back again and stormed off. I pushed up a slider on the huge sound desk in front of me and the boy's trembling voice sounded through multiple sets of speakers, "Should I start again?"

From a folding camp chair on the lawn in front of the stage a strained male voice called out through obviously clenched teeth, "No, no. Let's take a break. Tea break, everybody! Start again at 7.30 from the beginning of scene two. With our microphones turned on!"

"What a way to spend our Christmas holidays," my companion muttered as he removed his headphones and straightened his own beanie.

"Yeah," I agreed, stretching as I stood up from behind the sound desk, "but at least we're getting paid."

"I wouldn't be here if we weren't," Danny the lighting man replied as he disappeared over the edge of our raised platform and climbed down the scaffolding to the lawn below.

Alone on the platform, I slowly took off my headphones and looked out over the scene below. Two weeks previously the lawn had been a pristine part of the beautiful Mona Vale public gardens. Now it was a hive of theatrical activity with two huge towers of scaffolding carrying banks of lights and providing tenuous platforms for the crew that worked them. Black cables ran from their bases like tree roots, snaking across the lawn to smaller towers holding lights or speakers. Across the lawn were two stages; one a large fake castle with cardboard walls, the other one smaller with an equally fake hut including a door that led nowhere. A tiny stream meandered behind the stages, curving around the castle to feed into a large decorative lake, its edges festooned with flaxes and native plants that provided homes for the ducks and those funny little black scaups that spent most of their time under water. I watched one dive and counted to fifteen before it reappeared a metre from where it had gone under.

Slowly I scanned the groups of people in strange costumes who began appearing from the two large tents on the other side of the stream, wandering across the tiny bridge that spanned the stream and settling themselves on the lawn, cups of tea and coffee in their hands. I recognized the evil Sheriff of Nottingham by his bright purple cloak and waved to him and to the slovenly peasant woman he was talking to, then I scrambled down the scaffolding to join my parents.

"You look tired," Mum said, holding out a can of coke as I crashed on the grass beside them.

"It's crazy, I'm going insane," I replied between gulps.

"Problems?" Mum asked.

"It sounds fine to me," my step-father, Grant, added. "Apart from that little hiccup with young Tom."

"Young Tom will get more than a little hiccup if I get my hands on him," I muttered darkly. "He keeps playing with his radio mic – turning it off, pushing the mute button, playing with the batteries. He's a little brat!"

"Unfortunately, he's the president's little brat," Grant said pouring himself a coffee from a thermos he produced from a bag at his feet.

"Unlike in our own theatre company where you are the president's brat," added Mum, grinning.

"I have never been that awful!" I said indignantly. I might be turning into a vampire but that's different – and it doesn't show in public – yet.

"True," said Grant, answering my spoken sentence not the

one I was thinking, "but then you don't have Heidi McCormack for a mother. Her idea of discipline is to stuff another bar of chocolate in his mouth."

"Sad, but true," I agreed, flopping backwards on the grass. "I'm exhausted! Like I said, it's crazy. Props and wardrobe have got more assistants than they need while Danny and I are running around like headless chickens. His helpers are stuck ten metres in the air on the followspots and I'm by myself trying to operate the desk out the front and troubleshoot any problems out the back at the same time. If we were being paid by the number of times we climb up and down that tower we'd be sweet. I could do with two more crew – one backstage on radio mics and one willing to crawl under that stage every time we lose a connection. Have you got any food in that bag?"

"Taking a leaf from Heidi's Little Book of Brat Handling – have a chocolate bar," said Mum, throwing me a handful of Cadbury products. "You obviously fixed that squealy noise you had problems with yesterday," she added. "I presume Severn's email held the vital clue."

"Yeah, I now know a lot more about earth loops than I did before. But that's one of the things that make this so hard. I've only worked the sound board on one school production – I don't have the experience to rig and run this thing. I thought I was only operating the board – no-one told me that the usual guy was going away and leaving it all to me. I could do with Severn here, not on the other side of the world. It's not even our theatre company! Tell me again, when we could have been spending our holidays lying on a beach watching Grant burn sausages on the barbie, why we are here, getting burnt to a crisp during the day and freezing our butts off in the evening, watching Grant prancing around in a pair of green tights?"

"Because," said Grant sagely, "your mother is undoubtedly the best mezzo soprano in town and they couldn't resist my commanding presence or my fabulous legs."

"Speaking of commanding presence," I interjected, "I see the stage manager heading this direction, rounding up the troops. I'm off to find that monster child and gaffer tape his microphone before I head back up the tower. Bye."

"Hang on," said Grant, putting out a hand to restrain me as I rose, "leave me the gaffer and I'll deal with Monster Child. Mic on, mute off, batteries in, right?"

"Right. Thanks. See you later."

"She misses him more than she lets on, you know," I heard Mum say quietly as I walked away.

"Tough thing, keeping up a long-distance relationship," agreed Grant.

Oh yeah, you got that right!

CHAPTER TWO

17,500,000 sites, according to Google. I checked out the first three. Wikipedia said vampires were mythological or folkloric, were bloated and wore shrouds. Not the ones I know, mate! The ones I know are all skinny dudes in t-shirts. And if I am turning into one, the last thing I need is to be bloated. Exit Wikipedia. The next site had lots of pictures of people in black costumes snarling fake pointy teeth to the camera. Well, I can identify with the black clothes, especially for practical purposes back stage. The third site was more of the same so I gave up. Any more would just get boring. Plus, it's not as if it was the first time I had done the search. What did I expect to find anyway? A tourist link? "Spend a blood-curdling weekend in a medieval French monastery with a tribe (horde? swarm?) of real vampires." Or maybe a "So you're turning into a vampire – FAQs click here". I don't think so. I stopped day-dreaming and clicked back onto the unfinished email to my personal vampire.

To: Severn
From: Riley
Subject: 101 ways to murder bratty boys
RANT BEGINS. I am soooo pissed off – in a big way. We had the shittiest rehearsal yet. Danny and I are trying to get it through their thick heads that this isn't the same as an ordinary show. We're not in a theatre where we pack it all in then spend a week or so getting it right before the show starts – we're outside, running cables and gear across lawns and hanging it in trees, we have to pack it all away every night in case it gets stolen then spend another hour or so the next day running it all out again, so the problems we have today are completely different than the ones we had yesterday, or the ones we will have tomorrow. And there's only one of me. I fixed that earth loop, thanks for your advice there, but today I kept losing sound to the main speakers – I have no idea why – and that horrid child turned his mic off three times then broke the pins on the connector. Grant had to end up giving him his mic and shouting his own lines at the top of his voice. Then the know-it-all lead guitarist from the musicians yet again tried to be "helpful" by "neatening" the cables – yep, I know you've already figured out what I'm going to say next – the stupid

prat laid them all nicely side by side and then I copped the abuse when the dmx signals fed from the lighting cables into the sound system. Their committee called a meeting after the rehearsal "to discuss progress" - Danny tried to stick up for me but apparently I'm "head of sound" so I'm supposed to be able to fix it. I tried to point out that I am a 16 year old schoolgirl who has learnt enough about a sound board to know when to push the sliders up, but they basically said "tough luck – do it". There are so many other things on during the 'Summertimes' programme that all the professional techs were already booked – so I'm all they've got. Yay! This is NOT FUN ANYMORE!!! I should have taken Dad up on his offer – even with his horrid new wife and ugly new baby Australia would be BETTER! THAN! THIS! RANT ENDS

How's France? Is it cold? I saw on the tv news how it was snowing and flooding over there. I suppose you can't flood though if you're way up on top of a mountain. I've attached a picture I took on my phone today – just to make you jealous. The guys paddling in the lake are musicians. The director is the one in the awful towelling hat. I don't know the name of the lady in the multi-coloured skirt but she's been there every day so she must be wardrobe or make-up or something. Send me a picture of the snow from the top of your monastery. Tell me more about the strange little room you found. The place must be huge if there are whole rooms that people have forgotten about. Surely the Reverend must have known it was there.

Gotta go now – have to sleep. If it's nearly midnight here it must be nearly midday at your place so I guess you lot will have just had breakfast if you are all still on theatre-tech time???

Love you, miss you heaps, Riley

From: Severn
To: Riley:
Subject: Re 101 ways to murder bratty boys

Breakfast at lunchtime?? Cheeky cow!! I've been up and working since 6am thank you! Unfortunately. It's a monastery – they don't do sleeping in. In fact, they think 6am IS sleeping in!!! It sux. And yes it is snowing. Been snowing for 3 days solid. Snow sux! Yes it is bloody cold! The monastery has no heating at all. Some of the main rooms have open fires but even if somebody bothers to light them, the rooms are so big they don't make much difference and they certainly don't warm anywhere else. The older guys don't feel the cold but Aiden and I do. I guess we'll get used to it eventually but in the meantime we both look pretty strange with all the layers of clothes we have on. Today I can barely move as I am wearing thermals, jeans, t-shirt, sweatshirt, big woollen monk's robe with hood, and a ski jacket – plus fingerless gloves and a beanie!

The strange little room is apparently called the Redemption Chapel. Rev says of course he knew it was there – it's just that nobody has bothered to use it for the last 400 years or so. So now it's mine. Rev agrees it is an ideal spot to run the new computers from – we can put a satellite dish on the roof and it won't be seen over the parapets – can't have the locals thinking the monks have gone high-tech (even though we have). I will have to put a generator on the roof as well for the power but then I can have some heating as an extra bonus. I showed your pic to Rev and Aiden – we are all jealous, even if it does sound as if your show sux – they both say Hi. I've been thinking about your speaker problems – there'll be an email coming shortly from Rev with some ideas he's had.

Luv ya, Sev

CHAPTER THREE

Thrusting our trays before us like battering rams, Mum and I fought our way through the holiday crowds in the mall's food court, staked our claim to one of the few empty tables and tucked into our oversized muffins, spread with gooey white icing and a smattering of yummy raspberries. I pushed the froth on my cappuccino around with a teaspoon.

"I hate it, Mum," I confided. "I never thought I would hear myself say that I hated doing a show, but I am truly beginning to hate this one. Without Grant's rubbish about his no-way-sexy legs, why are we doing it?"

"Well," said Mum, sipping her coffee delicately, "the City Council called for tenders from theatre companies wanting to supply the outdoor show and we decided to give it a go. Then we discovered a) how expensive it is to run, b) how much money you could lose if the weather turned nasty and c) that the Mad Hatters wanted to do the same show. Grant cunningly suggested that, instead of taking all the financial risks ourselves, we should just support them in their tender – so we did and so they got it and we are tagging along, supposedly having all the fun without the hassles – although I gather it is becoming the other way around with you."

"It sure is. It was fun for the first couple of weeks but then their sound guy went away and I was left all by myself – then everything started to go wrong and I have no idea how to fix some of it. I can't believe they were so mean last night, basically saying it was tough luck. Surely they could find me someone else to help. What if I tell them tough luck and quit?"

"I hope you won't – although I must admit that I wouldn't blame you if you did. Between you and me I've come close myself once or twice. Don't tell Grant I said that."

"Why? I mean why did you want to quit, not why shouldn't I tell Grant. I thought you guys were enjoying yourselves?"

"We are, most of the time. But that Heidi McCormack is a Grade A bitch. You would think she was the star of the show the way she acts – even though her part is even smaller than mine – and Grant is the Sheriff while her husband is only the King who doesn't come on stage till the very end – but her husband is "THE PRESIDENT" so she thinks she can push everybody around.

"But your husband is "The President" of our company and you're not horrible to people."

"That you, my dear, I try not to be. I think of us as all taking turns and doing our best to make things work for the good of the show. Heidi, on the other hand, thinks the sun shines out of her own bum and that we should all kiss it whenever she approaches."

"I thought the sun was supposed to shine out the bum of her bratty monster."

"I'd like to slap the bum of her bratty monster," Mum agreed. "But I think I would have to stand in line behind the rest of the company, stage manager first."

"Me first – she can take her turn if there's anything left of him."

Mum laughed. "Enough poisonous talk – let's cheer ourselves up with a bit of heavy-duty shopping. It's a lovely day and because the set builders want to strengthen the steps behind the stage with no actors around to get in their way, we've got eight glorious hours before we need to be back at Mona Vale so where shall we start – clothes or shoes?"

It's one of the things I like about Mum – she takes shopping seriously and she has great taste in clothes. We staggered out of the mall two hours later with two pairs of trousers, three tops and a pair of new boots each. Mum also had a pair of pink open-toed, high heeled shoes and a huge floppy hat and I had new trainers and a wide silver bracelet. Power shopping, Mum called it. We both felt much better and ready to tackle Mona Vale and the Adventures of Robin Hood.

As we pulled into our driveway, Grant straightened up from the garden he had been weeding and by the time we had unloaded our parcels he had the electric jug boiling and the coffee mugs set out on the kitchen bench. I was about to take my coffee down to my room when the phone rang. Grant answered then handed it to me.

"It's Australia. Your dad."

I grimaced, but took the phone as there was no way I could get out of it.

"Hi, Dad. How's it going?"

As I spoke to him I watched the expressions on Mum and Grant's faces. They could only hear my side of the conversation and, although I was tempted to turn it to speaker phone, I knew

Dad would hear the change and it wasn't worth the hassle. I knew that Mum could figure out what he was asking from my replies.

"No, Dad, I am not coming over to Australia next week.... I told you I am running the sound desk in a show.... no, I can't leave it to someone else.... I don't want to even if I could.... I know you have a new baby.... yes, I realise that she is my sister (Mum smiled at the face I made).... you called her what? Is that a real name? .... I said no, Dad.... not these holidays.... not a chance.... oh, for heaven's sake, Dad, it is not a plot by Mum to stop you seeing me.... I am busy.... okay, okay, I will try to come at Easter – how does that sound? .... yes, I realise the baby will be bigger then.... so what?.... I would rather wait till it's bigger... sorry, till SHE is bigger.... I don't like little babies, I'd probably drop her.... sorry, Dad, but that's my final offer – Easter or not till way later in the year.... oh, don't give me that 'don't see you very often' rubbish – you're the one who chose to stay in Australia. If you want to see me more often you could move here, or at least pay the airfares.... yeah, yeah, whatever.... bye, Dad."

I hung up and banged the phone down on the bench.

"Arrgghh!! As you probably gathered, he expects me to drop everything and rush over there just so he can show off his new toy."

"She is your half sister," Mum said calmly. "Don't you want to meet her?"

"Not particularly. I am not a huge fan of babies. I might like her when she can walk and talk, but right now – no, don't care. Mind you, I feel a bit sorry for her – poor little thing is going to look like either him or her, or a cross between them. And I don't feel like rushing across the ditch just to goo over something that probably looks like a monkey."

Still angry, I stamped around the kitchen, muttering swear words and making myself a second coffee which I managed to spill over my hand. That was the final straw! I screamed, swore, threw the coffee mug into the sink, where it promptly broke, and then remembered enough about burns to realise I was supposed to have my hand in cold water. Ten minutes of cold water on my hand and Mum fussing in my ear was enough to calm me down.

"What are you really angry about?" Mum asked as she picked the broken mug out of the sink. "Or can I guess? Is it because your dad doesn't see you very often and you miss him, or because he has a new girlfriend and now a new baby and you feel left out?"

"Left behind, more like," I admitted. "It's like you and I were a nuisance and he was glad we left, but now he has a new family and they are exciting and he likes being with them. I hate him!"

"But he obviously wants to include you," Mum reasoned. "He keeps on begging you to go over there."

"Yeah, right! I'm not sure if that is so he can gloat or so I can be a handy babysitter so they can go to the pub. I am not going!"

"Fair enough – it's your choice. You can always wait till the baby is older and has her own computer and you can talk to her on webcam."

I laughed, apologised for breaking the cup, threw the broken pieces into the rubbish bin, made a third coffee in a new mug and took myself off to my bedroom to think. With the stereo playing loud "thinking music", I fired up my computer where, hopefully, there would be an email from Severn to cheer me up. There wasn't. But there was a lengthy email from the Reverend with his troubleshooting tips for the speakers, so I printed it off and prayed that I wouldn't need it because everything would go right tonight.

CHAPTER FOUR

As if! But it wasn't just my department – everyone seemed to be having a bad day. As we pulled into the carpark we could see Danny kicking the door of the large container that held all the technical equipment. I opened my door and heard him swearing. Grant raised his eyebrows.

"I wonder what's eating him?" he asked. Pulling on his happy face, Grant stepped out of the car and walked confidently towards the container. "What's up, Danny? Got a problem?"

Too angry to speak, Danny pointed. We got the message. Someone had backed their car into the side of the container, bending the door just enough to jam the mechanism. Danny aimed another futile kick. Grant hunted in the car boot till he found a tyre lever which he took to Danny and between the two of them, with a lot of grunting and groaning, they managed to bend the door back into shape. A bit more heaving and shoving and it finally opened. That disaster over, Mum and Grant helped us unpack the gear out of the container onto the two big trolleys we were using to push the gear across the lawns to the stage.

Danny's two followspot operators arrived as we were loading the trolleys so with their help the next hour disappeared in a blur of cable-laying – around trees, up trees, through trees, under the stage and up the scaffolding tower. By the time everything was plugged in and actually appeared to be working, I was hot, sweaty and dirty. Did I say that this was NOT FUN! Still I was reassured by the fact that noise was coming from all the speakers and all the microphones tested okay. I should have known it wouldn't last.

The musicians arrived. The theatre company has some wannabe-famous band from the posh high school on the hill and every day we went through the same ritual. They would set up their gear then complain because the mix wasn't right. It had only taken me two days to figure out that this really meant that each of them wanted to play louder than the guy beside him, so I quickly got very good at nodding and waving from the sound desk and pretending to turn dials. End result – they were happy and the sound levels were exactly where they had been before we started the daily nonsense. Hmm, maybe I really was getting good at the job. As they declared themselves happy I picked up a radio mic, flicked on its channel, panned the channel to put my voice through the musician's foldback speakers and threatened the guitarist with very specific examples of extreme bodily harm if he touched a single one of my cables tonight. It might not have achieved anything but it felt good.

But if my day was starting okay, Danny's wasn't. Two of his lights had blown bulbs so his crew were climbing up and down the scaffolding like monkeys while Danny was muttering about budgets and complaining about getting replacement bulbs. I got out of their way by heading backstage to deliver the radio mics to the actors in their makeshift tent dressing rooms.

In the ladies' tent Heidi McCormack was delivering a grand speech that no-one was listening to. I caught something about "professionalism" and "setting the correct tone for family viewing". Her accent fascinated me. I've got used to the difference between New Zealand speech and my own Australian vowels, and I can tell the difference between the actors' every-day accents and their rounder on-stage voices, but hers was something else again. She managed to sound as if she was rolling plum stones around in her mouth and imitating the Queen of England at the same time. As she continued to rant, I began to feel sorry for the rest of the Mad Hatters Theatre Company. If they had to put up with her all the time, why did they stay? I filed it away in my brain to ask Mum about later – maybe she could poach a few for our company when the show finished. I looked around and spotted a couple of the ladies from our company who were, like Mum, helping out in this show. They did not look too impressed with Heidi's behaviour. Like most of the other women they were changing into their costumes, doing their make-up and making faces to each other behind Heidi's back. Mum was putting on false eyelashes and trying not to laugh. As Heidi finally ran out of breath and turned her attention to applying a hideous shade of red lipstick, I got on with my job. When the lead characters all had the transmitters for their tiny wireless microphones safely tucked into the cloth packs they wore under their costumes, the wires run up their backs and into their hair and the tiny lavelier microphones taped to the edges of their cheeks, I headed over to the men's tent to repeat the exercise over there.

Because of the way the little stream meandered through the site, to get to the men's tent I had to cross over a temporary and rather dodgy bridge made of a couple of wooden planks. I stopped and looked down the stream before I dared to cross the wobbly contraption. At the back of the stage I could see the stage manager and her crew checking the pieces of set and off to one side the wardrobe lady was hanging costumes on a rack for those actors who had quick changes and wouldn't have time to go back to their tents. Looking the other direction I could see one of the lighting crew checking a light on the small second stage while a couple of guys dressed as Robin Hood's Merry Men looked on. Tommy the Wonder-Brat was with them. He was supposed to be waiting in the tent for me to come and put his mic on him. I so hate that kid.

Feeling a bad temper coming on, I stormed over the bridge to the men's tent where, at least, everyone else was where they were supposed to be. Grant raised his eyebrows at my grumpy mood but didn't say anything. Just as well as I might not have been polite back. Even the usually pleasurable task of taping a mic to the impressively built body of the leading man failed to cheer me up, and the men picked up on it enough so that they didn't make any of their usual rude comments as I threaded the wire down the back of his trousers. "You don't look happy," was the leading man's only comment.

"Good spotting! Now all I have to do is find that little monster and tape this mic so far up him he will have to be a contortionist to get to the mute button."

"Not too far up, if you don't mind," Rob, the leading man, laughed. "I have to take it off him and hand it on to Alice for Act 2 and I don't fancy fishing it out of where I think you are suggesting putting it."

"Well, if it got stuck there, then maybe his father would get enough extra crew on board so we could have a specialist fisher-outer back here and you wouldn't have to get your hands dirty," I sneered.

"15 Minutes!" came over the speakers. Damn, I'm running out of time. And I still have to find that snotty kid!

Snotty kid was still down at the second stage, leaning on a tree talking to the woman in the flouncy, multi-coloured skirt. She had her hand on his shoulder and was smiling at him like he was the star of the show. Which he thought he was. She glared at me when I butted in.

"Hey you!" I couldn't be bothered being polite. If he wants to complain to his daddy, great – bring it on! "You were supposed to be at the tent to get your mic on. It's not my job to have to find you. Take your shirt off, turn around and shut up!"

Not giving him any time to complain, I grabbed him by the shoulder, spun him round and set about attaching his mic pack in the very centre of his back where I hoped he wouldn't be able to reach it.

"It's not comfortable there," he whined.

"Tough!" I retorted.

"I'll move it for you," weird-dress woman offered.

"No, you will not!" I hissed at her in as low and menacing a tone as I could manage. "I don't know who you are. I don't know if you are wardrobe or make-up or one of the gardeners but I sure as hell know you are not on sound, so you will not touch any of my equipment. Do you understand?"

She was about to reply when the 10-minute call came over the speakers.

I raised my finger to them both. "Touch that mic and you die!"

Still fuming, I ran back to the tower and climbed the scaffold to take my place behind the sound desk.

CHAPTER FIVE

Once the rehearsal got started, I began to calm down. I seemed to be the only one not having major problems. Danny was still muttering away beside me, swearing repeatedly into the comms to his operators who I could hear swearing back. On stage it wasn't going any better. The director yelled at actors for forgetting their lines, the musical director yelled at the musicians for playing too fast, the stage manager yelled at the crew for stuffing up scene changes. Finally we staggered to the end of Act One and the director called for a break. It was now nine o'clock. Act One should only take 50 minutes but with all the stuff-ups and repeats it had taken double that. It was now dark and getting cold and we still had Act Two to go. It was going to be a long night.

I was just about to take off my headphones and leave the sound desk for a break when I heard the stage manager's voice asking if Danny and I were still listening.

"Yep," we both replied at once.

"What's up?" asked Danny suspiciously.

"The director wants four more microphones across the front of the main stage, two more speakers and an extra lighting tower in the far right corner," the stage manager ordered.

"You are kidding!" Danny was not impressed. "What the hell for?"

"He wants more light on the fight scene and the chorus without radio mics aren't being picked up and can't be heard unless they are standing beside someone with a mic on," the stage manager replied.

"Well tell him he sure as hell isn't getting it tonight," Danny growled. "I can't pull a lighting tower out of my backside." He snapped off his comms, ran his hands through his grey hair, looked at me and shook his head. I must have looked like a stunned goldfish.

"I don't even know where to get more microphones. And I haven't got any lines left on the desk to plug them into," I felt crushed. "Or speakers. Their sound guy got this gear – he brought it in before he left. What am I going to do? I can't do this." I burst into tears.

"Oh crap," said Danny. "I'm going to talk to the president." He took off down the tower.

I fished a hanky out of my pocket, dried my eyes and blew

my nose. Crying was not going to help. But I still had no idea what to do. Maybe Mum and Grant could help. The sound operator from our own theatre company was out of town touring with a fashion show but if Grant could get hold of him, he could at least tell me what to do.

Then my cell phone vibrated in my pocket. I hauled it out and stared at it blankly. A message from a withheld number. Curious, I opened it.

"angels r us look up look left"

I looked up, peered through the darkness of the encroaching night. Looked left – towards the carpark. And they were there. Three figures emerged out of the gloom, striding side by side like the baddies in a b-grade western or the chorus-line for a musical version of the Matrix, long black coats flowing behind them. Before I could get out of my chair the one in the middle had broken into a run. I have never climbed down the scaffold as quickly, but I was still not at ground level when he reached me, picked me off the scaffold and pulled me into his arms.

When I came up for breath I could see Mum and Grant standing up from where they had been sitting on the grass and walking towards David and Aiden, hands outstretched in welcome.

"What? How? When?" I stuttered, wrapping my arms around Severn's waist under his coat as we walked to join the others.

"Sounded like you needed help," Severn smiled, his arm around my shoulders.

"And we needed sun," Aiden added.

I gave him a quizzical look. "You? Needed sun? Umm…?" The "have you forgotten you're a vampire?" question left unasked.

"Oh no, not in the want-to-hang-out-in-the-daylight way. We were just sick of snow. It is so cold in the mountains."

"And we were bored," the Reverend added. "Sounds like we got here just at the right time. We were in the carpark. We heard the director's little request."

Of course they did. A normal person sitting beside me wouldn't have heard it unless they were wearing headphones but of course the vampires heard it. I wonder how long it takes for things like that to change – my hearing hadn't changed at all yet and it had been three months since I had drunk Severn's blood and started the change-over. I must ask them how long it takes and what the symptoms are.

"How did you get here so quickly? I only emailed you yesterday?"

"We flew," Severn replied with one of his pedantically correct and obvious answers, complete with raised eyebrow over his fine, tortoiseshell-rimmed glasses.

I gave him a similar look back. "Flew? Um, flew... as in...?"

"As in the Lear Jet," Severn laughed. "You weren't thinking...?" and he flexed his shoulders so I could feel his wings move under his t-shirt. "We are not that fast – or that fit."

"Weren't you worried about coming back so soon after ... what if they stopped you at the airport? Don't the police still want to talk to you about the body at New Brighton?"

Severn smiled and pulled a passport out of his coat pocket. I looked at the name – Benedict Bailey. The passport was French.

"Benedict Bailey?" I whispered. "Is your passport guy an alcoholic or something? You left here as Father John Benedictine on a Vatican passport, now you're named after two types of drink, not just one." I shook my head in disbelief. Severn laughed.

"So who are you in public? Severn or Benny?"

"You could just yell, hey you. That could work."

"Riley!" Danny came up behind us. "I've spoken to the stage manager, to the president and to the director but got no-where. We have to find all this extra gear tomorrow and make it work. Sorry. I am going to be struggling just to get my lighting stuff. I will ask around to see if anyone can help with the sound stuff, but I can't promise anything."

"Sorted." The Reverend stepped forward. "I'm David Rochester. We've worked with Grant's company before and we heard yesterday that Riley was struggling, so we've come to help."

Danny tilted his head to the side quizzically and looked down at the diminutive figure in the enveloping ankle-length coat. I could tell what he was thinking. The Rev was even shorter than me with long hair pulled back in a pony tail. He looked like a doll. Danny gave Severn and Aiden an equally hard appraisal that seemed to last for ages before breaking into a wide smile. He grabbed the Rev's hand and shook it firmly. "Welcome aboard. Any of you do lighting?"

"We all do," the Rev replied. "We're a professional crew, we all do everything."

"Oh halleluiah! That is the best thing I have heard all week! Let's talk later. In the meantime, Riley, they want us at our desks.

Act 2."

Severn joined me at the sound desk and I was happy to let him tweak the dials as his super-sensitive ears picked up all the faults in the mix. He couldn't fix the faults in the acting. As the hour got later, the actors got more and more tired and made more and more mistakes until half way through the act the director called it quits. Which was fine for the actors, but Danny and I still had about an hour's work packing up all the gear and stowing it back in the container. Well, an hour's work without three strong vampires. With them the pack-out was just finishing as Mum and Grant arrived in the carpark.

"Where are you staying?" Mum asked.

"We've booked a motel a couple of blocks from your place," the Rev replied.

"Can I go with them?" I asked.

Mum smiled. "Of course. Just… um… oh," her hands flapped as she struggled. "Just for coffee. Don't stay out too late."

I knew what she wasn't saying but was thinking

The motel lady's suspicious look said that she was obviously thinking the same thing. I guess we did look a bit strange. All in black, none of us looking older than teenagers and arriving close to midnight. Still, she handed over the key to the unit and pointed out where we could park the guys' rental car. Inside, the unit was really nice – two bedrooms, a bathroom and a lounge with a tiny but complete kitchen. Severn grabbed the room with the queen-size bed; the Rev and Aiden making rude comments as they threw their bags on the two single beds in the other room. Then over cups of coffee I filled them in on my disasters and they outlined their plans to fix them. Tomorrow they would all source and pack in the extra gear, including helping Danny to rig his tower, then Severn would take over the sound desk, Aiden and I would do radio mics and the Rev would trouble-shoot all other disasters. I stopped panicking. From now on the show was going to be fun.

I had lots of questions for them too, but Aiden had been twitching and pacing the room all through the talk about the show and had started to make pointless, grumpy comments to every suggestion. The Rev kept calming him down but was having less and less luck and Aiden was getting more and more obnoxious. So, reluctantly, I suggested that Severn should take me home. It was nearly two o'clock in the morning and I was exhausted, so even though I really wanted to stay with Severn, I knew that going home was the right decision.

Severn drove me home and pulled into the driveway. As I unclipped my seatbelt, he pulled me close. His kiss was rough, hungry, almost brutal. I wanted to pull away but I wanted it never to stop. I kissed him back just as hard. Our hands moved over each other, finding their way under the layers of clothing. I slipped my hands around his back, feeling his wings tremble as I ran my finders down their furled ridge. He moaned, pulling me tighter. I knew he wanted to turn the car around and drive back to the motel, to the queen-sized bed, and part of me wanted him to do just that. Then a light came on in the house and I knew Mum and Grant were waiting up for me. I also knew that when I got inside they would pretend that they weren't, that it was just coincidence that they happened to wake up when I arrived, but that wouldn't be true. The knowledge that they were hovering, probably peeking out through the curtains, spoiled the moment and, suddenly, instead of enjoying the kiss, I felt like the whole world was watching. I pulled away.

"I think I had better go," I explained, pulling a sad face.

"Yes, I guess so." Severn sounded annoyed. "I think you are expected."

So, with mixed feelings of elation and frustration, I let myself out of the car and ran up the drive to the front door, which opened magically as I approached.

"Oh, hello," Mum failed to sound genuinely surprised. "I thought I heard something – must have been the car. I guess I don't have to ask you if you've had a good evening. See you in the morning. Good night."

As she walked off down the passage towards her bedroom, I could hear her softly singing something that sounded suspiciously like the theme from "Lost Boys", her favourite vampire movie. Sometimes Mum is just plain creepy!

CHAPTER SIX

Mum smiled at me over her breakfast toast.

"That was a nice surprise, wasn't it? Did you know they were back in the country?"

"Not till they walked in. They were in France. Severn was setting up some computers and Aiden was complaining of the cold. Apparently the Rev made some comment about the long email he had sent me, something about it being quicker to do it himself, and they made a snap decision to do exactly that."

"How did they get here so fast?"

"Private plane. Their company has its own jet."

"Oh, that explains how they got Severn out so easily after the Tasha/Dilys thing. It must be a big company. I thought they were just a small New Zealand-based group. Seth Borman must have been wealthier than he looked."

"No, actually they're part of an international company. That's why they're in France at the moment. David's in charge of things now." That's the short version of the explanation but it was all Mum was going to get. I still had no proof that she knew Severn was a vampire, although I really think she knows, but I certainly wasn't going to ask her. Not yet anyway.

What she didn't need to know was the rest of the story. A few months ago, when my classmate was killed backstage at a show, I had fallen in love with a member of the travelling professional stage crew who were working on the show, only to find out that he was a vampire. They were all vampires. Not pretend vampires with pointy, plastic teeth. Real, undead vampires who drank blood and flew on big, creamy, leather wings. And she definitely did not need to know that I purposely drank his blood, so now I was going to turn into a vampire too. Not a good conversation to have over breakfast toast.

If she knew they were vampires, it would be easy to explain how David is called the Rev by his friends because he is one. The Reverend Father David Rochester only looks like a teenager. He is, in fact, a 700 year old monk and he owns the medieval monastery the vampires use as their headquarters. Aiden and Severn had gone back to France with him after Tasha was killed – or rather Aiden and David got Severn out of the country quickly to stop the police dragging him into the police station and discovering his wings. Severn is the youngest of the vampires – he's only a hundred and twenty nine.

"Hello! Earth to Riley!" Mum's voice cut into my thoughts. I shook my head to clear it and smiled at her.

"Sorry, I was miles away."

"Oh gosh!" Mum clapped her hand to the side of her face in a mock gesture of shock. "I never would have noticed. I wonder why."

"Was that sarcasm or bad acting?" I retorted before grabbing a piece of her toast and taking a determined bite.

"Oooh, oooh, oooh," Mum replied giving a left-right-left shoulder shrug as she laughed. "That was my best Heidi McCormack impersonation. I am miffed that you are not overwhelmed. So, what are your plans for the day? What time should I expect the Men in Black?"

I shook my head as I swallowed the toast. "You really are seriously weird sometimes." I looked at my watch. "Oh heck, soon! The Rev has a whole bunch of ideas for getting the extra gear, so we will be collecting it then meeting Danny at Mona Vale to get it all rigged. That means I have got about twenty minutes to shower and dress then I will be gone all day and won't see you until you get to rehearsal."

"Clean blacks are in the clothes drier. While you were gallivanting around with three strange men last night, I was slaving over the washing machine."

"Thanks, Mum."

I hauled myself out of the dining chair and headed off to the bathroom. By the time I re-entered the kitchen, dressed in my backstage gear of black jeans, black t-shirt and black Doc Marten boots, the "Men in Black", as Mum called them, had arrived and were all seated comfortably around the kitchen table, drinking coffee and chatting to Mum. Severn looked up as I walked in and smiled. My heart melted. He leaped up, pulling me to him for a kiss which I was just beginning to really enjoy when the Rev broke us up.

"Enough of the schmaltzy stuff you two. We have serious work to do."

We dutifully sat down – Severn on the chair and me on his knee with his arms around my waist. The Rev waved a piece of paper in the air.

"I have made a list of the supplies we need and where I

think we can get them from. Watch and learn!" He pulled out a cell phone from one of the many pockets in his coat, which he never seemed to take off even when he was inside, and dialled. "David B? David R.... yes, it's been a while.... yes, we are back in town.... Robin Hood, Mona Vale.... yes, that would be one word for it.... how did you guess.... the director has had "new ideas".... yes, we all know what that means.... can you supply an eight or twelve channel desk, four speakers, as much cabling as you can spare .... yes, I am planning on daisy chaining them together.... and microphones - four turtles and a couple of shotguns.... Fantastic! Also, what have you got in the way of lights – parcans and floods.... yes, an extra dimmer pack would be awesome. Where can we collect them? .... How soon? .... Great, see you there."

He hung up and beamed at us. "Done! Everything we need. All we have to do is get out to Oxford to collect it all."

"Oxford?" Aiden looked puzzled. "That's in England, isn't it?"

"Yes and no. This Oxford is just over the Waimakariri River and down the road a bit." The Rev looked at our enquiring faces. "That David is an old friend I met years ago in England. He moved out here a while back and brought all his sound and lighting gear with him. Very handy chap to know – if he hasn't got it, he can probably make it on the spot. Aiden, what I need from you is a van big enough to carry all this stuff. Can you call the car hire firm please?"

"I can do better than that." Grant's voice came from the doorway. "I've got a couple of friends with vans, let me call them and see if I can borrow one."

One phone call later we had a van on the condition that Grant drove. Leaving Mum behind sorting costumes, we all piled into the rented vampire-mobile and set off to pick up first the van, then the equipment. It was a bit squashed with three people in the back seat of the car, but I wasn't complaining. I certainly wasn't complaining when we swapped the car for the van as it had three seats in the front – Grant and Rev with Aiden in the middle, a black cap pulled down over dark glasses – leaving the small folding back seat for Severn and me – cosy! I snuggled up close to Severn and enjoyed his presence beside me, the softness of his sweatshirt and the hardness of his muscles underneath it. It's quite a long drive from Christchurch to Oxford, through lovely, classic New Zealand countryside with awe-inspiring views, but today the views didn't matter and the journey was too short. I was leaning against

Severn, eyes closed, enjoying his fingers running gently through my hair, then we've stopped and the Rev is telling us we have arrived, so get out and start loading. End of a lovely moment!

Still, the gear was perfect. Danny would be impressed. David's friend, the other David, helped us load it all into the van and it wasn't long before we were on the road again.

Danny met us in the Mona Vale parking lot, almost jumping for joy. He had done his part as well and already I could see a crew of scaffolders erecting the new lighting tower. At the sight of the lights being unloaded from the van, he actually clapped his hands in delight and did a little happy dance on the spot, yelling "Wahoo" and "Onya". Severn gave me one of those looks he gives by bending his head slightly and looking over the top of his glasses, which translates as "What the…?" and Aiden failed to stifle a laugh.

"Let's get this stuff in the air, then the beers are on me," Danny offered, stroking the nearest light like it was a favourite puppy.

"You're on." Grant grabbed an armful of cables and headed towards the lawn where the stage was set, with the rest of us collecting anything we could carry and following like sheep.

"Stella for me," Aiden put in his order.

"Speights," Grant threw back over his shoulder.

"Tui."

"Steinlager."

The debate about beers expanded to include the scaffolders and continued on and off for the rest of the day as the tower grew, the lights were hung, microphones were set along the front of the stage and new speakers positioned. Aiden, still sporting the cap and glasses and not saying much, and I ran cables while Severn and the Rev set up the second sound desk, moved all the microphones to the biggest and allocated the new, smaller desk solely to the equipment for the musicians. The plan we had made last night changed slightly - I would now be mixing the sound for the musicians while Severn worked the large board, leaving the Rev and Aiden floating backstage sorting out actors and other problems. So now, instead of running around backstage watching Severn from a distance, I would be sitting right beside him – gee, not a problem.

CHAPTER SEVEN

Even the stage manager was impressed. As the evening got darker the true value of vampire stage crew began to show – even if I was the only one who knew why they were so good. One of the first things that made me realise there was something different about Severn and the Rev, way back last year when I first met them backstage at the show where my schoolmate, Tasha, was murdered and for a while Severn got the blame, was the weird way they could be here one second and somewhere on the other side of the theatre a few seconds later. At first I couldn't figure it out. I would be talking to them in the alley outside the theatre, then I would go back inside and they would be back at their stations while I was barely through the stage door. Or the way the Rev would hear things I said when he was upstairs and I was backstage. It wasn't until I saw the Rev and Aiden in the theatre one night, shirts off, with their huge, creamy, leather wings flying them up to the lighting rig, that I realised they were vampires. Back then I freaked out but a lot had happened since then. Now it seemed normal that they could see and hear things going wrong before anyone else noticed, then suddenly appear in just the right place to fix the mistakes. It had to seem normal – I had drunk Severn's blood. Now I was turning into one of them. It was soon going to be my normal – for ever.

As I said, the stage manager was impressed. She singled out Grant at interval, asking where they came from. Grant told the truth as he knew it. That they were professional stage crew who travelled around as needed, that they had been employed by our company last year and that they had stayed in touch, so when they heard I was having problems they came to help. For no charge, he added before the stage manager could ask.

If the stage manager was impressed, Danny was ecstatic. After high praise from the director at the end of the rehearsal, Danny kept his word and as soon as the last of the gear was safely packed away into the container, he hauled a dozen of beer out of his car boot. I don't actually like the taste of beer but I wanted to fit in with the guys, so I took one and sipped. It was ghastly. My face must have given me away as everyone burst out laughing. Fortunately the Rev rescued me, pulling a can of coke miraculously out of his voluminous pockets and swapping it for the beer.

We all stood around for a while talking technical stuff, most of which went right over my head, and cracking bad jokes. When there were no beers left, Danny suggested that we go to McDonalds for food. Great idea - I was starving. I glanced at Severn and the Rev to see what they were planning and caught a look flash between them. They were hungry too, but not for the sort of food we eat. All of a sudden I was overwhelmed by the other reality of the vampires. I had seen them before, luring a drunken guy from a pub into a dark alley, taking turns lowering their mouths to his throat and sucking his blood from his body before discarding him on the ground like the empty beer bottles. As the Rev started to make their apologies, claiming they wanted to get some sleep, which I knew was a total lie, I felt sick. And terrified. How long would it be before I had to join their hunting sessions? I must have gone pale as Danny noticed and asked if I was all right.

"Yeah, yeah, I'm just tired and hungry" I replied quickly. "Can any of you give me a lift back to Linwood if I come with you to McDonalds?"

"Sure," the youngest of the followspot operators offered. "I live in New Brighton, so it's on my way."

I smiled a thank you, threw "See you tomorrow," over my shoulder to the vampires and walked off with the lighting guys. I'm sure Severn noticed that I didn't give him a hug, or a kiss, but right at that minute I was so revolted by what they were about to go and do, I would have been sick if I had touched him.

"My name's Cameron," my new friend introduced himself as we headed to his car.

"I'm Riley." I looked at him and smiled. Taller than Severn, broad across the shoulders while Severn was slim, blond hair, big blue honest-looking eyes and genuinely about my age, not just looking it and actually being a hundred years or more older. How come I hadn't noticed him before?

He had a boy-racer car. Lowered, pimped, tinted windows, mag wheels, noisy engine. It was just a couple of blocks from the Mona Vale carpark to the McDonalds in Riccarton Road but by the time we got there I knew more about the car than I cared about. Make, model, engine capacity. Nissan, GTI – R Pulsar, 1600 cc. It meant absolutely nothing to me – do people really care about those things? But I must admit that the car did look hot with its raised grill like a cheese grater in the middle of the bonnet. Cameron talked so much that I didn't have to do anything except nod my head and grunt occasionally, which was good as there was way too much running around inside my brain to leave any room for normal conversation. Where were the vampires going? Who were they hunting? I shook my head to get the pictures out and tried to concentrate on my new friend.

Over a cheeseburger and fries, upsized to large, I learnt that the other followspot operator was called Neville, that he was Cameron's uncle and that they had both known Danny for years. When it was their turn to ask me questions about Severn, Aiden and the Rev I made sure that I put something in my mouth just as they asked so that I would look like I was being polite and not talking with my mouth full, but actually I was thinking of how to say as little as possible without seeming obvious. I saw Cameron grin slightly when Danny pointedly referred to Severn as my boyfriend, so I smiled back, watching his grin change to amazement when I told them about the three arriving in their private Lear jet.

The idea of Severn having a bigger and better toy than his boy-racer car must have got to Cameron as I think his driving was supposed to impress me. It didn't. He drove too fast. Hard on the accelerator, harder on the brakes, the car's turbos whooshing and sneezing as he negotiated the one-way system back to our side of town. By the time we pulled into my driveway, I was beginning to feel sick.

"See ya tomorrow," Cameron called cheerfully out the window as he raced away, engine revving wildly.

I wobbled up to the front door, feeling queasy as I hunted in my pocket for the door key. Mum and Grant, who were watching a late-night movie, looked up as I walked in.

"Hello, you're earlier than I expected," Mum smiled.

"Yep, the boys needed sleep – jet-lagged," I lied. "I went to McDonalds with the lighting guys."

"Oh – right. I thought that wasn't their car."

I wasn't planning on getting into a long conversation about my ride home, so I said goodnight and hurried to my room where I pulled off my outer clothes, threw them in a pile on the floor and crawled into bed. Too many thoughts tumbled around my brain. Blond boy racers competing with sexy vampires. Sexy vampires competing with blood-sucking, hunting vampires. Where were they right now? Did I want to know? Eventually I fell asleep, one day closer to joining their ranks.

CHAPTER EIGHT

I slept late, wandering out to the kitchen in the middle of the morning. Mum looked at me over the pile of baking ingredients strewn over the bench.

"Good sleep, dear?" she asked.

"Yeah," I nodded, scooping chocolate cake mix out of the mixing bowl with my finger and licking it off.

"What are your plans for the day?" Mum asked innocently. "When are the boys due?"

"Oh, they're not." I switched on the jug and spooned instant coffee into a mug. "I expect that they will sleep all day and meet us at Mona Vale later." I couldn't explain that I knew about their hunting patterns. I knew that, having hunted all night and fed well on some poor victim, they would sleep till it was dark again. Sure, yesterday they had spent all day in the sunshine but I knew they didn't do that very often and they needed time to recover before they would do it again. Severn had explained last year that it wasn't that they couldn't go out in the sun – they just worked better in the dark, but a day in the sun after a trip halfway across the world and a huge change of time zones, added to a night's hunting, was bound to have them lying low for a few hours. Mum stopped spooning the cake mix into a cooking tin and waved the wooden spoon at me.

"So what are you going to do with yourself till five o'clock?"

"I thought I would go and see Anita. She texted me yesterday but I had to put her off, so I had better catch up with her today. I thought I would bike over to her place."

"Okay. But be back here by three, then we can have something to eat before we go to the show."

I wasn't in a hurry so it was about an hour later that I finally sank onto the end of Anita's pink, fluffy-bunny-covered bed. I love Anita, she's my best friend. I've known her since we first arrived back in New Zealand from Australia. At school she's as big a disaster in the science lab as I am, so we have a lot of fun. The science teacher hates us. I am sure that one day he will have a mental breakdown in the class and it will be our fault. The best thing about Anita is her complete refusal to grow up. While everyone else is wearing the latest fashion, or at least in jeans, Anita dresses in cute pink skirts and collects fluffy toys. Rabbits mostly. Her room is wall to wall fluffy bunnies.

"What's up?" I asked. Then I looked at her properly and realised that she looked worried. Not the usual happy Anita. "What's wrong?"

"No, no, nothing," she said quickly, but I could tell that wasn't the truth. She pretended some enthusiasm. "I'm bored and starved of gossip. Tell me some. You're backstage at a show, you must have some juicy goss on someone. Spill!"

She didn't need to ask me twice. Over coke and chocolate biscuits I told her about the show, the ghastly problems with the technical stuff and then, at great length, the even ghastlier problem of Heidi McCormack and her hideous little creep of a son. Anita munched one biscuit after another as I spoke, stopping only to nod and refill her coke glass. As we opened our second packet of biscuits, I got down to the important stuff.

"Severn's back."

"What?" Anita choked on her coke. "When? How?" she spluttered over a coughing fit.

She laughed as I described their dramatic arrival at Mona Vale, coats flying out behind them. Then she wanted a run-down on everything that had happened since and I ended up telling her about Cameron the boy racer.

"What?" she choked on her coke again. "Are you crazy? You have a boyfriend to die for and one day after he rushes from the other side of the world to be with you, you're chatting up another one?"

A boyfriend to die for – bad choice of words, Anita. A boyfriend I am slowly becoming immortal for, more like. But I can't tell her about that. I wish I could – I desperately need to talk to someone – but "oh, by the way, I'm becoming a vampire" is a difficult line to throw into a conversation, even with your best friend.

"I wasn't chatting him up – he was doing all the talking. It wasn't anything – I only went to McDonalds and then got a ride home. It's not like a date!"

Anita sternly waggled a chocolate biscuit at me.

"Keep it that way. Don't you dare stuff up what you've got!"

What I've got – I'm not sure if I want all of what I've got. The nice bits, yes, but the immortal-sucking-blood part I can do without. I was so busy thinking about vampires that I almost missed Anita's bombshell.

"I'm pregnant," she said so quietly I thought I had misheard.

"What? Who?" I was so shocked I could hardly speak. Not Anita of the fluffy bunnies! Not possible! I didn't even know she had a boyfriend – she was better at keeping secrets than I was.

"Caleb."

"Caleb? Chemistry nerd, plays the violin, rides a yellow scooter Caleb?"

Anita nodded.

"Bloody hell! How long have you been...you know...?"

"Just once. I went with him to last year's school dance. You didn't go, remember? It was just after the Tasha thing and Severn wasn't around and you said you didn't want to go with anyone else, or by yourself, so you stayed home. Seeing you weren't going, I had no-one to go with and I didn't want to look like the class loser walking in by myself, so when Caleb asked me to go with him, I said yes. He is a bit of a nerd but he doesn't look too bad. He actually turned out to be fun. He's got a wicked sense of humour. Anyway, he had a bottle of water, except it wasn't water, it was vodka. I got really drunk and we did it in the school garden behind the staffroom. It took about five minutes, I got scratched from the rose bushes and then threw up on the daffodils. Now Caleb is following me around with his tongue hanging out hoping we will do it again, which we won't, and I'm going to have a baby in August. I don't know how to tell Mum and Dad, they'll kill me."

"No they won't. They might be angry for a bit, but you have to tell them. They won't stay mad for long and, let's face it, you're going to need their help if you're going to keep it."

"What do you mean if? Of course I'm going to keep it! What else would I do?"

"Well, you could always adopt it out."

"No! I would spend the rest of my life wondering if it was okay. It's my baby and I'm keeping it."

"Yeah, okay." I grabbed the last biscuit. "What are you going to call it? Bunny?"

CHAPTER NINE

I was really glad I wasn't running the sound at the show any more. Because if I had been, everything would have fallen apart. I had so many things running around my brain competing for thinking time I completely failed to concentrate on what I was supposed to be doing. I was on auto-pilot, running cables along the ground from the speakers back to the desk and wondering why there didn't seem to be enough cables when we had plenty yesterday, when Severn appeared soundlessly beside me, spun me gently around to face him and asked what was wrong.

"Nothing," I said quickly.

"Yeah, right! Try that again." He pulled me down to sit on the grass. "Something's going on. Have I done something to make you mad? You dashed off last night like you were pissed off with me about something, you didn't text me all day and now you're wandering around here like a zombie, making all sorts of mistakes. So spill! What's wrong? What have I done?"

I put my head in my hands and gave a huge sigh.

"Nothing." He raised his eyebrows and gave me one of his looks over his glasses but I continued. "You haven't done anything to piss me off. Well, you probably did, last night, but that doesn't piss me off, it just freaks me out." I looked at him, grabbed his hand and squeezed it hard. "It's not zombies, but it is this whole undead vampy..." - I was trying not to say the word - "...thing. I'm not freaked out that you guys are, I'm not at all freaked out by the flappy wing thing – that's actually quite cool, but I am freaked out about what you have to do ... to ... ah ... um ... to feed," I finished lamely. "Last night I knew where you were going and why and it just did my head in. Especially as I don't know anything about how long it takes to change into one of you since I did, you know, the biting-drinking thing in the theatre. How long is it going to be before I have to go with you and do that too? That scares the shit out of me."

Severn pulled me to him in a hug, softly holding my head against his shoulder. I felt peaceful for the first time all day. He rested his cheek on the top of my head.

"I'm sorry. I should have thought. I guess it is all pretty weird for you. We've all had a long time to get used to it. It is hard at first. I thought I would go crazy. There were a few times when

I wished someone would come along with a sharp stake and kill me, so I get that you're freaking out. Just trust me, it will all be okay. Whatever happens, I will be here, and so will the Rev and Aiden. They are pretty protective of you, you know. I bet you didn't know that Aiden followed you last night when you went off with lighting boy, just to make sure you got home safely."

For a split second the thought of being followed made me really, really angry. If Aiden had been standing there I probably would have slapped his face. How dare they do that! Then, just as quickly as it had flared up, the anger disappeared and I saw the funny side. The boy racer trying to impress me with how fast his car could go and right behind him, keeping pace in the dark, my own security vampire. I burst out laughing. Severn lifted my face in his hand, smoothed back my hair and gave me a gentle kiss, followed by a longer, delicious one that I didn't want to end. But it did.

"Come on," he said, pulling me to my feet, "let's get these cables sorted. What the hell were you doing with them?"

I looked at them and felt really stupid.

"Oops. Now I see why I thought we didn't have enough. Daisy chains." I slapped myself on the side of the head. "Dumb cow. They are supposed to be going from speaker to speaker to speaker, not each speaker back to the desk. Duh!!"

Severn laughed, called Aiden over to help and between us we quickly fixed my stupid mistake before anyone else noticed. Well, I hope it was before anyone else noticed. As we walked back to the scaffolding tower that held the sound desk, I caught sight of Cameron watching me from high up on his tower, behind his followspot. Anita was right – what the hell was I thinking! I put my arm around Severn's waist and snuggled into his side. Eat your heart out, Cameron, you've got no chance.

Up on our tower we made ourselves as comfortable as possible, although not as comfortable as I would have liked. With Severn working the big desk and me on the smaller one, there was too much distance between us to allow us to touch each other, but not enough that I wasn't really aware of him sitting beside me. He must have felt the same as between cues he would look over at me and smile, or wink, or reach over and share his chocolate bar. I couldn't see Cameron in the dark, but I knew he could see us. Occasionally I wondered what he was thinking, but I didn't care.

Again, with the vampires doing their technical magic, the

rehearsal went really well. Aiden was a huge hit with the ladies in the women's dressing room – they were almost fighting each other to have him fit their radio mics. Even Heidi McCormack was charmed. The Rev dealt with the men and he was exactly the right person to handle dear little Tommy. Mum and I had figured out ages ago that he didn't listen to 'grown-ups' but as the Rev was shorter than me, long-haired and looked like a teenager, Tommy the Brat didn't know what to make of him so he was shocked into doing what he was told. The Rev looked so innocent but delivered his commands in a voice so cold it would freeze a penguin. It worked. Little Tommy stood nicely to have his mic fixed, left it alone and even said thank you. Score points for the Rev!

Finally, as the evening got cold enough to make me shiver, the show ended, the director gave the cast his notes on what they had done wrong and we climbed down from our towers ready to pack up and go home. While the actors rushed off to the dressing room tents to get out of their costumes, we stormed through the pack-out, coiling cables and carrying gear as fast as we could. With the last of it stowed away, Danny slammed the container door shut and suggested McDonalds. Cameron grinned. I tucked myself under Severn's coat, wrapped my arms tight around his waist and waited to see what the vampires would answer. Would they come or would they be desperate to get out hunting again tonight. Severn gave me a squeeze in reply.

"Yeah, sounds good," he replied to Danny.

"You don't have other plans?" I mouthed at him almost silently, knowing he would hear with his vampire ears but the lighting guys wouldn't.

Severn bent down, scooped me close and whispered in my ear. "I might later, but not what you're thinking. My plans involve you and me and nobody else."

I was sure Severn could hear my heart beating, it was going so fast.

"I'll text Mum, let her know I'll be late."

"Very late."

I pulled out my phone and started to text when Mum and Grant walked into the carpark with a group of actors and wardrobe ladies. I noticed the strange woman who wore the multi-coloured skirts following behind them, just far enough back that I still couldn't work out if she was part of the wardrobe department or not. I put away my phone, ran up to Mum and told her that I was going to McDonalds with Severn.

"Okay, dear," she smiled. "Have fun."

And with that, they were in their car and off, followed out of the carpark by a stream of other cars. The McCormacks were the last to leave. Tommy was throwing a temper tantrum about something, Heidi was trying to bribe him into submission with yet another chocolate bar and the promise of an icecream on the way home. Mr McCormack just looked exhausted. He had obviously come to the rehearsal straight from work as he ignored Tommy's tantrum, got into a different car and drove off. As Heidi struggled to get her darling screaming little boy safely seatbelted into her car, over behind a tree the weird woman stood watching. At least, I thought she was watching, but I could have been wrong as, when the drama was over, she wheeled an old-fashioned bike out from behind the tree and rode off. Maybe she just found it all as fascinating as I did – our daily dose of bad soap opera – who needs Shortland Street, we've got The McCormacks.

And I had way more important things to think about. McDonalds first, then Severn – all to myself.

CHAPTER TEN

McDonalds was a drive-through. The lighting guys went inside but we did a quick drive-through and then back to the vampire's motel. For a while we all sat in the lounge eating burgers and talking about the rehearsal. Aiden brought up little Tommy's temper tantrum and the conversation quickly sank into a dramatic recreation with Aiden starring as Tommy and the Rev as Heidi. I nearly wet myself laughing.

"So why do people put up with the little horror?" Aiden asked when everyone had calmed down again.

I explained how his father was the company president.

"And that's mother – the loud, bossy woman who thinks she's the star of the show?"

"Yep, that's Heidi."

"Heidi?" Aiden roared with laughter again. "Heidi! Like the milkmaid? Ja, my name ist Heidi," he broke into a fake German accent and started skipping around the room, twirling his hair in his fingers and batting his eyelashes, "I am a wery cute little milkmaid mit long, blonde hair, ja!"

"Idiot!" I said, thinking that I would never be able to look at Heidi the same way ever again.

The conversation calmed down after that, but Aiden didn't. For the next half hour he twitched, paced, fidgeted and generally annoyed the rest of us until, finally, the Rev stood up, grabbed their coats and, with a quick, "See ya later", pushed Aiden out the door. I wanted to ask what Aiden's problem was, but I figured it was a vampire thing that maybe I didn't want to know about. Maybe he didn't get enough to east last night, or maybe he had too much, or maybe the sun was getting to him. But I wasn't game to ask Severn. If they were going hunting but Severn wasn't going to mention it, neither was I. Best not to know. Anyway, I had a whole different lot of thoughts running through my head.

Severn barely waited for the door to close before he made his move. His arm curled around me, pulling me to him, leaning in for a kiss. On my lips first, gentle and loving, then harder and stronger, more determined, his tongue probing inside my mouth. At first I responded. It felt wonderful. I could feel my heart and my breathing speeding up. I wanted him to keep going. I thought of the kiss in the car, and how much I had wanted it to continue, how I had wished we were here, in the motel. So why, in the back of my mind, was something not right? I pushed back the picture of him feeding and concentrated on the passion of his kiss. Then his right hand slid inside my t-shirt and began to make its way up my body, under my bra. My body reacted instantly, arching towards him, wanting more. As I kissed him back, he moved fluidly, scooping me up and moving me from sitting to lying on the couch, his body over mine, his hands suddenly everywhere, stroking and kneading. My body responded even though my brain was sending random "watch it" messages which I was trying to ignore. An image of Anita, pregnant, flashed through at one stage but I squashed that thought – hadn't Severn explained how vampires can't make babies? I was here with a gorgeous, sexy male – this was not the time for thinking!

It was the bite that killed it. His kisses had moved from my lips to my face, my ears, my neck. Then the kisses became a gentle running of teeth across my skin. Then a nibble, a sharp intake of breath and a small but sharp bite. That did it! Body seized up in shock. Brain took over.

"Stop!" I said breathlessly, trying to push him off me but failing. Severn pinned my arms down gently but firmly and tried to kiss me again.

"Stop!" I said again, louder this time. I began to struggle to get out from underneath him.

"It's all right," he murmured, "it's all right." His tone of voice was one I hadn't heard before, soft and almost hypnotic. "You're safe, you'll enjoy it."

Now I was angry! I pushed him away with all the strength I had, rolled out from underneath him and leapt to my feet.

"How bloody dare you!" I shouted. "I said stop. I meant stop. Stop does not mean keep going. I want to go home. Now!"

His reaction wasn't what I expected. I don't know what I did expect but I think I expected him to say sorry, not to get all shitty back.

"Oh for f***'s sake!" he swore as he flung himself off the couch to stand over me, hands on my shoulders holding me in place, face full of anger. "What did you expect? I got the impression you were raring to go. We all got the impression you were hanging out for it – why do you think the other two went out and left us alone? I told you I had plans and I'm bloody sure you knew exactly what I meant, but you still came here, you didn't run home with Mum. So what's your problem?"

My problem was that, all of a sudden I had realised that I wasn't on a cosy date with a boy from school – I was alone in a locked room with a horny vampire. We had been giving one of the girls at school heaps for going out with an "older man" who was twenty two, and here was I almost doing it with a guy who only looked eighteen but was actually nearly one hundred and thirty! How many times and with how many women had he done it? Plus the biting thing. I didn't want to be his tasty snack, thanks. And they had planned it! Not only was Severn expecting me to sleep with him, he had organised it in advance with the Rev and Aiden. Bloody hell!

"You planned it!" I said. "You guys had it all figured out. Well, sorry." I forced myself to calm down a bit. "I'm sorry," I repeated, waiting as his breathing slowed and his anger faded. "I'm sixteen. I've never done it. You're what? A hundred and twenty something? You probably know exactly what you're doing. But I don't. It was all a bit fast. And a whole lot too planned. Sorry. I'm sorry if I gave you the wrong message. I'm not even sure I know what the message was but obviously what you were picking up wasn't what I was putting down. And … and you tried to bite me!"

Severn managed to look apologetic at that.

"Sorry," he said, the grip on my shoulders lessened from holding me in place to a gentle squeeze. 'You're right. I got carried away. I guess I did get the message all wrong." He turned away, breathing heavy determined breaths, obviously calming his anger and his frustration. Then he reached for my jacket, handed it to me in silence and pulled on his long, black coat. "Come on, I'll walk you home."

We walked silently through the Linwood streets. I don't think either of us could think of anything to say, although I did let him put his arm around me. It felt comfortable and I wished it could have stayed like that, instead of where it had just gone. Now I was even less sure of where it would go next.

I let myself quietly into our house, made myself a hot chocolate and crawled into bed.

CHAPTER ELEVEN

By the next morning the shit had hit the fan. I had slept late. It had taken me ages to get to sleep and I had strange, horrible dreams that kept me tossing and turning but that I couldn't remember after I woke up. I remember seeing my bedside clock say 3:47 but I must have dropped off properly after that as it was nearly ten o'clock when I finally made it out to the kitchen, still in my pyjamas, hunting for breakfast. As soon as I walked into the room I realised there was a problem. You could feel the panic.

"Oh, hello, dear, did you have a good evening?" Mum asked in a vague tone that showed she really wasn't going to hear any answer I gave.

"Yeah, lovely." Safe answer. "What's going on?"

Grant put down the phone he was holding and stopped rifling through the phone book to ask, "Tommy McCormack. When did you see him last?"

"Last night, as we all left Mona Vale. Heidi was trying to get him into his seatbelt and he was throwing a temper tantrum. They were the last out of the carpark just after you and before us. Why?"

"He's missing. His father phoned us this morning. Apparently Heidi stopped at a service station to buy him an icecream, left him in the car while she ran into the shop and when she got back to the car he was gone."

"What? He ran away? Well, he was in a stink of a bad mood. He's probably spent the night under a bush somewhere and will turn up at home this morning, all sorry for himself."

"That's what we're all hoping. But we're not so sure."

"Why?"

"They were only three blocks from their house. Tommy knows the way to and from the service station – he goes there all the time to buy lollies, so he would have known how to get home, even in the dark. No matter how angry he was, he would have got home by now. Plus, Heidi said that he had given up on his temper tantrum and calmed down. He was looking forward to his icecream as she had promised him the new variety they've been advertising on tv, so he wouldn't have run away – not till after he got his icecream, anyway."

"So what do they think happened? Do they think someone kidnapped him?"

"That's what Heidi thinks. Apparently she started screaming as soon as she saw the car door open and no Tommy. The service station attendant called the police when he couldn't calm her down, then the police called an ambulance and they had to sedate her. I'm not sure what the police think but apparently they're taking it seriously. It's been on the news this morning and the tv showed pictures of the police dogs sniffing around the service station."

"So what's going to happen to tonight's rehearsal?" Mum broke in. "Heidi and Angus are going to be a right mess if Tommy hasn't been found, plus there's the problem of who's going to do Tommy's role. I mean, it's a dress rehearsal – it's kind of important. We can't just not have it but we can't have it with three people out of action."

"I'm sure he will turn up by then," Grant soothed. "And even if he doesn't, the show must go on and all that. Angus doesn't come on till the very last scene, so one of the Merry Men can fill in there easily. I'll give Jocelyn from our group a ring and warn her that she may need to read in for Heidi. Tommy … I'm buggered if I know but I've got to phone the director back soon and I'm sure we'll think of something between us."

As if on cue the phone rang. Grant answered, waved his hands to indicate that it was the director, then took the phone into the lounge leaving Mum and me in the kitchen nursing our coffee mugs.

"So how was your evening?" she asked again, obviously forgetting she had asked that already.

"Not as good as I had hoped." Truth was the easiest option this time. "We had a bit of a misunderstanding." Okay, not all the truth.

"You had a fight?"

"No...yes...sort of."

"Oh."

"It's not a problem, Mum. There's just stuff we need to sort out." Less truth, more rubbish, thinking quickly. "He lives in France, I live here. He has a job, I'm still at school. You know, stuff like that."

"Yeah, right." I thought of the Tui beer advertisements where "yeah, right" means exactly the opposite. She didn't believe a word I had just said. "More coffee, Mum?" Change the topic. "So how come Grant's all involved in the Tommy thing? Did they think he has him stashed away in the garage?"

"No, silly," Mum laughed. The phone's been going crazy all morning. Heidi and Angus have rung everybody and everybody is ringing everybody else. Grant is just doing what he always does in emergencies – taking charge and putting things in order."

I thought back to the last time Severn was in town and to how Grant had saved the day at the last moment by diverting the police to the wrong side of town. Yes, for someone who looked so helpless he was surprisingly good at fixing things. Although I must admit that he didn't look helpless when he came back into the kitchen.

"Sorted," he smiled. "Herr Direktor will read in for Tommy, at least for tonight. Susan," he turned to Mum, "he thought it would be a good idea if you could go around to the McCormacks and keep Heidi company."

Mum pulled a face. "Do I have to? I can't stand more than a minute of her at the best of times – she'll be ghastly!"

Grant gave her one of the looks he gives me when he expects me to do something he knows I think is horrible but I can't get out of. It worked.

"Oh, all right," Mum gave in. "But I'm not staying all day. I have things to do."

"Oh heck," said Grant, admitting his role in giving Mum a shit job. "I'll come too. Angus will be just as upset as Heidi."

So that just left me, all by myself, to think about last night and what did and didn't happen. I made myself some toast which I munched on automatically as I wondered what Severn was doing. What was he doing right now? What had he done after he brought me home last night? Had he gone hunting? Whose blood had he sucked? The only thing that sucked for me was that I couldn't talk to anyone about it. Not even Anita. What if we had done it? What would it have been like? Would it have been wonderful, like a tv show couple, or would it have sucked, like Anita's drunken few minutes in the school garden. She must feel like shit. I couldn't do anything about stupid little Tommy, who I didn't give a rat's arse about anyway, but I could maybe help my best friend. I decided to get dressed then give her a call. But that didn't happen either.

I had pulled on some non-backstage non-black clothes, blue jeans and a purple top, and was cleaning my teeth when the door bell rang. I quickly rinsed the toothpaste out of my mouth and made it to the door just as it rang again. I pulled it open to be greeted by a huge bunch of bright yellow daffodils and behind them, holding them with the downcast look of a lost puppy, Severn. He looked so pathetic I laughed.

"I'm sorry," he said quietly. "I really am. Really. Sorry. Am I forgiven?"

"Oh, come in," I giggled, taking the daffodils from his outstretched hand. "Of course you're forgiven. But we probably need to talk about a few things."

Severn released his hold on the flowers, stepped forwards and pulled me into his arms. We kissed. Everything was all right again. The world was perfect. I forgot about Anita.

CHAPTER TWELVE

How come every time I have a sexy vampire in my house we end up sitting in the kitchen eating toast and drinking coffee? What does that say about me?

Severn apologised so many times I had to keep kissing him to make him shut up. I put the flowers in a vase and put them in the middle of the table. I knew Mum would ask about them as soon as she saw them, but she liked romantic ends to stories so she would love that he had said sorry. Severn asked where Mum and Grant were and I told him about Tommy. He was actually interested. And a bit freaked when I said that the cops had been called in. We agreed that if they showed up at Mona Vale, he would quietly disappear; after all there was still the problem of his fingerprints at a murder scene in Dunedin over forty years ago – he couldn't afford to have the police look at him too closely. Then we agreed that we were being over-dramatic and that Tommy had probably turned up by now, demanding chocolate.

"If he hasn't maybe that's how they could find him," Severn suggested. "They could lay a trail of chocolate bars and wait for him to follow them."

"Oh ha ha. Still, they must have found him by now – the service station will have security cameras so they should at least know which direction he went, and with the police dogs, surely he can't have got that far. Enough of brat-boy. I have vampire questions." Time to get down to the real stuff. "How long does it take?"

"How long does what take?"

"Changing over. Back last time you said that the only way to change over into a vampire wasn't if a vampire bit you, it was when you drank the vampire's blood. And I did that, back in the theatre, so you could fly. So now I figure that I'm turning into a vampire. Which freaks me out big time. And I haven't got a clue what to expect. I mean, Anita, my best friend, she's just told me that she's pregnant." Severn looked at me wide-eyed. "And that sucks, but at least she knows how long it's going to take. At least she knows she's going to get huge in a few months then have the baby in August. I haven't got a clue what to expect. When will I grow wings? Are they tiny to start with? How do I hide them when I go swimming? When do I start drinking blood? When do I have to start going hunting with you? How do I go hunting if you guys are in France?"

I was babbling, starting to panic as all the questions tumbled out of my mouth.

"Whoa, slow down." Severn came to me and pulled me out of my chair into his arms. "Slow down. Everything will be okay. Let's go through one thing at a time."

I leant my head against his chest, feeling safe as he stroked my hair. I could feel his breath softly ruffling against the top of my head.

"What can I expect?" I asked. "How long before it starts? What will I notice first?"

He moved his hands to my shoulders and held me away so he could look into my eyes.

"To be perfectly honest, I don't know. We probably need to talk to the Rev."

"How can you not know? It happened to you?"

"Yeah, but," he paused then continued, "slightly different. Mine was a rush job. It wasn't voluntary. I was tied down, sucked out till I was almost dead, then made to drink a huge glass of Seth's blood every day for a week. So it happened quickly. But the wings took longer. It was only a week or two before I was dragged out hunting with them but it took a month or so before the wings started to grow, then about five years before they got full sized, and, if you remember, I still couldn't use them. Actually, I don't think they were full sized even then – I'm sure they've got bigger since I've been flying regularly."

I looked up at him in surprise.

"Flying? Regularly? For real?"

"Yep. That's the benefit of living in an old monastery miles from anywhere in the French mountains. There's nobody to see us except maybe the odd farmer, but they don't tend to go out after dark and on the rare occasion that they do see us, they think we're angels."

"Angels?"

"Yep. The monastery is called Montagne des Anges, Angel Mountain, and there have been vampires living there for hundreds of years, so if someone sees something winged flying over the monastery roof, they just cross themselves and call it an angel. Very handy for us."

"I guess. Until some modern kid with a cell phone takes a

pic and puts you all on the internet."

"Oh, I hadn't thought of that. Still, nobody would believe it, they'd say it was photoshopped."

"True. But, back to my questions. So I am still confused and you have no useful answers. Correct?"

"Correct, sorry."

"You're apologising again."

"Sorry."

"Stop that or I will be forced to kiss you again."

"Sorry," he grinned.

So I did.

CHAPTER THIRTEEN

By the time Mum and Grant arrived back from their visit to the McCormacks, we had also been joined, or interrupted, by Aiden and the Rev, carrying pizza boxes and, believe it or not, garlic bread! We had demolished most of the pizza before Mum and Grant walked in and they quickly grabbed the last few slices.

"Oh, yum, I needed that." Mum gave a contented sigh as she bit into a piece.

"No sign of Tommy, then?" I asked.

"No. Not a word. Heidi is a complete mess. The doctor came while I was there and sedated her again. The police came and have left a woman liaison officer at the house but there's not a lot she can really do. It got to the stage where there wasn't anything useful I could do either, so we left them to it."

"Angus doesn't know what to do," added Grant. "He's feeling helpless and Heidi doesn't help as she is rejecting everything he tries to do to help her. So I agreed with your mum – best we left and concentrated on keeping the show going this evening."

"What can we do to help?" the Rev asked.

"Just keep on doing what you've been doing for the last couple of days. That way, at least we know the technical side of the show will run smoothly."

"Consider it done," the Rev replied. "In fact, let's get ahead of the game. We'll go over there now and get set up early, then we can triple check it all before the actors arrive. Come on, girl," he aimed at me, "get into your blacks and we're out of here."

"Okay, give me five minutes," I replied.

"Do you want a hand?" Severn asked innocently.

"No!" Mum, Grant, the Rev and I all said at once. Aiden sniggered.

Even without Severn's help I was changed and back in the kitchen in under five minutes. Well, my speed was more probably because I didn't have his help – with it, I doubt that I would have got past the taking off of my blue and purple clothes and we never would have made it to the putting on of my black ones. I grabbed some muesli bars to stuff into my jacket pocket along with my beanie and we were out the door.

At Mona Vale the extra time made the setup fun. Instead of

rushing around trying to do six things at once, we were able to take our time and lay out everything perfectly, checking and re-checking till we were certain that there would be no problems with the lights or sound. Danny had the same idea about arriving early, but his idea of early didn't match ours and we were running the final checks when he pulled in. The look on his face said it all.

"Hey, guys," he smiled. "You doing my job for me? I'm liking that a lot."

"Yes, we're done," Aiden smiled back, a top-lip only smile that showed just a hint of white, pointed teeth. "And we've still got two hours before the rehearsal starts. What are we going to do?"

"Lie in the sun," I suggested, but that got a negative glare from all three vampires.

"Go to the pub," suggested Danny.

"I can't do that, I'm not old enough," I protested.

Danny looked us all over studiously. "Doesn't look as if any of you are old enough. Okay, compromise, I'll go to the pub and bring the beers back – and a coke for you, Riley."

"And we will find a shady tree to lurk under," added Aiden. "Out of the sun!"

We carried on tidying up the cables till Danny returned with a six-pack of beer and a large bottle of coke, then we settled under the biggest shady tree and made ourselves comfortable to wait for the actors to arrive. Danny started the conversation with the obvious question.

"Any word on the boy?"

"Don't think so," I replied. "He hadn't turned up when we left my place and if they'd found him since then, Mum would've texted me."

"Bloody hell! What sort of a pervert would steal a kid from his mother's car?"

We all just looked at each other and fidgeted because nobody had an answer. I mean, for real, what sort of a pervert would steal a kid from his mother's car?

"I guess a father might, if they were fighting over custody or something," I finally suggested, more to break the silence than because it was a good answer.

"True," Danny observed. "But that's not the case here, is it? Angus and Heidi are never going to be in that situation. I've known them for years – Angus was in my class at school. Heidi latched onto him at a school dance way back when we were about your age." He pointed to me. "She knew he was a good catch then and she's certainly not going to let him go now he's a successful businessman."

"Have they got any other children?" the Rev enquired. "I mean, if they've been together since they were at school, is Tommy the baby of a line of them?"

"No," Danny replied. "Just the opposite. They didn't have much luck at first. They tried for years to have a baby and we all thought they had given up. Heidi even got herself a job in a little florist shop over in Fendalton. Then one year she chucked that in, announced that she was pregnant, Angus took some time off and they went on an extended holiday to their Wanaka holiday house for a few months, then arrived back in town complete with bouncing baby boy."

I was about to say that it must make it even harder for Heidi losing him when my mind took a jump to the left. Babies – Anita. I was going to call her to see how she was. I pulled out my cell phone to send her a text.

R u ok hv u tld ur mum. C u 2moro

I pushed my phone back into the pocket in my jeans and looked at Severn.

"Do you want to come for a walk?"

He squinted up at the sun through the tree and screwed up his nose, then he shrugged.

"I guess. As long as it's shady."

I grabbed his hand and we hauled each other to our feet, looked around and chose ourselves a winding pathway leading off through the trees that surrounded one side of the tiny lake. He put his arm around my shoulders and pulled me tight to him as we walked. I could get used to that.

"Before," I began as we strolled, "you said that your changeover wasn't voluntary. So what happened? Where are you actually from and how come you ended up with Seth Borman and the Rev?"

"Once upon a time," Severn laughed in a sing-songy voice, "there was a boring little farm boy from a boring little pig farm outside a boring little country town that is now only a 40 minute drive from the edge of Edinburgh but back then was a whole two days' horse ride away." His voice dropped back to normal. "I was bored shitless. I hated the place. My mother died when I was about five and my father did nothing except tend the pigs and go to church. Then, when I was fifteen, he slipped when he was feeding one of the sows – a huge, nasty piece of work she was. I wouldn't be surprised if she had pushed him over. Anyway, before he could get up and get out of the pen she turned on him. I was in the barn. I heard him yelling but by the time I got there she had bitten him badly – there was blood spurting everywhere. I tried to get him out but it was hopeless. I ran into the house, grabbed the shotgun and shot her but it was too late for Father. He was dead. After the funeral I just walked out. Never been back."

He paused for breath.

"I didn't know pigs were that nasty," I said. "I thought they were pink and cuddly."

"This one was black, white and vicious. I hate pigs."

"And then you met the vampires?" I prompted.

"Yeah, sort of... with a gap of a couple of years in between. I walked all the way to Edinburgh and lived rough for a while. Got jobs wherever I could find work. Then one day a circus came through town. That's when I met the others. I was looking for work and they were part of the crew. It took me a lot longer than you did to work out that there was something different going on with them. Olivia bit me first. I wasn't supposed to remember it the next day but I did. I didn't tell her that I remembered. I wasn't sure if I had remembered or if I'd dreamed it. So I waited to see what would happen next and if she would do it again. She did. And I remembered it again. Then I started following them and watching. I had no idea what they were as you don't tend to learn about vampires on Scottish pig farms. I couldn't figure out what they were doing, or why. And, of course, as I had no idea how good their hearing is, I got caught by Seth. When I said that I had been watching them, and I knew Olivia had bitten me, Seth was furious. He wanted to kill me on the spot. I was lucky that Olivia and the Rev stood up to him. Thinking back, it was the Rev who suggested that I be turned. Somehow they got Seth to agree although he wasn't happy. But they had to do it quickly because the circus was moving on. They kept me in Seth's caravan until it was over and there was nothing I could do but go along with it. Hmm, I said before that I was lucky that Olivia and the Rev stood up for me – maybe I was unlucky. It's certainly way different than pig farming."

"So how come you're now a computer nerd?"

"Guess I was smarter than I knew. And you learn a hell of a

lot when you've been around over a hundred years."

"I guess you do." I paused. "How come you haven't got a Scottish accent?"

"Practise. How come you've still got an Australian one?"

"Practise."

CHAPTER FOURTEEN

By the time we had completed the whole circle of the winding garden track, including stopping a couple of times to kiss and cuddle, the actors were arriving for the dress rehearsal. The atmosphere was completely different to normal. Instead of rushing off to their dressing room tents to get ready, people were milling around on the grass in front of the stage like a flock of sheep, asking each other questions and swapping ideas of what might have happened to Tommy. There was no sign of the McCormacks. Mum and Grant were in the thick of the mob, steering people in the right direction and generally taking charge.

"Ah, there you are," Mum greeted me as we walked up to them. "Anita rang. I told her that you were here so she said to ask you to go and see her tomorrow morning. She also said that she had no credit on her phone."

I felt guilty.

"Is she all right?" Mum asked. "She sounded stressed."

"As far as I know," I lied. "I'll ask her tomorrow." I grabbed Severn's hand and walked away, trying to look purposeful and not like I just wanted to stop talking.

"Anita," Severn caught on. "Didn't you say she was pregnant?"

"Shhh! Yes, but Mum doesn't need to know that yet."

"Riley!" the director's voice cut across the lawn, breaking into our conversation. I turned to face him as he strode towards us. "Riley, can you please set me up with a microphone – I want to talk to the cast and crew before we start."

"Sure, come on Sev, you grab a mic and I'll turn up the channel."

We sprinted to our scaffolding tower and quickly attached a microphone to the director's shirt collar. As he strode to the centre of the stage, I turned up his channel so he could address the mob of human sheep milling in front of him.

"Okay, everybody, can I have your attention please?" he began, then launched into a disjointed ramble about the missing Tommy, throwing out words like "tragedy" and "support" and even "show must go on" before naming the two regular actors who would replace the McCormack parents, saying that he would read in for Tommy and asking me if he could, therefore, keep his microphone. Sorry, mate, we haven't got any spares, you'll get one delivered when you need it, be grateful you won't have to shout.

"This is still a dress rehearsal!" he ended. "We open in two days! So please, please, no matter how bad we feel for the McCormacks, remember we must all concentrate. Give the best performance you can! Now go, everyone, get changed and made up. Curtain up in twenty minutes!"

The cast members scuttled off obediently to their tents as the crew, equally obediently, clambered into our towers or headed backstage. Twenty minutes later, on the dot of seven thirty, the stage manager's voice came over the comms and the rehearsal was underway. The next couple of hours went by in a blur of cues, coke and chocolate, the latter out of the endless supply from the pockets of the Rev's coat. Maybe he has shares in Cadburys. Somehow, by the end of it all, the director was pleased. We climbed out of our towers, packed all the gear back into the huge container and staggered, exhausted, to the cars. Mum and Grant were sitting in his car, waiting for me.

"Coming with us or going with Severn?" Mum asked.

I smiled ruefully at Severn. "Sorry, I'm so tired, I think I'll go home. Plus I've promised to see Anita tomorrow morning so I can't sleep in."

Severn shrugged a non-committal reply but gave me a long, not-non-committal kiss. That would do. I climbed into the back of the car, lay my head back and almost fell asleep on the ride across town. It had been a long day. Once home, we all stumbled in the door. I went straight to my bedroom to change into my favourite pyjamas while Mum made for the kitchen. Over comfort food of hot chocolate and toast, we picked the rehearsal apart then turned to the news of the day – the missing Tommy. Grant had turned on the tv to catch the late news and Tommy was the third item. We stopped talking to watch as a policeman explained how they were studying footage from the service station cameras but there were still no definite leads. There were some shots of the outside of the McCormack's house and even a shot of the empty stage at Mona Vale.

"Hmm," said Grant as he switched the tv off. "I guess any publicity is good publicity."

"You're not suggesting they've made this up to publicise the show, are you?" Mum asked, horrified.

"No," Grant laughed. "Even Heidi's not that obsessed. I just meant, that last shot, of the stage, they mentioned the show, so even if they come out of curiosity, it won't hurt the ticket sales."

"Trust you to think of that," Mum admonished.

"That's gross," I added.

"I don't know, it could be good," Grant argued. "If Tommy turns up safe and gets back on stage, think of the crowds who will flock to see him. He'll be as famous as he likes to think he is."

"I can't believe the police don't have any leads," Mum said.

"I'm sure they do," Grant answered. "They just aren't telling the reporters. If they're looking at someone, they won't want to warn them."

"I just feel so sorry for Heidi," Mum said. "It would be horrible losing a child." She looked at me. "If I had lost you like that, I would have gone mental."

"Especially when they waited so long to have him," I said.

"Did they?" Mum sounded surprised. "I assumed they married late."

"No, apparently they've been together since school." I told Mum the story Danny had told me earlier. Mum agreed that it explained a lot about why Heidi spoiled her son rotten.

As I settled into my bed a few minutes later, I briefly wondered if Anita would be like that about her baby.

CHAPTER FIFTEEN

Tommy's photo was all over both the morning paper and the tv news. He still hadn't turned up. Although she didn't really want to, Mum decided she should do the right thing and visit Heidi. I reminded her that I was biking over to Anita's so we agreed to meet at Eastgate Mall for lunch and the promise of some shopping. I figured Mum must be more worried about the Tommy thing than she was letting on – she always eats muffins and shops when she's stressed. Great – I had an awesome day to look forward to – a stressed Anita and a stressed Mum. Yay!

Anita was super-stressed. It made me feel even more guilty for forgetting to talk to her yesterday.

"Have you told your mum yet?" I asked as soon as we reached the privacy of her toy-infested bedroom.

"Yes, I told her the day before yesterday," Anita replied, clutching a purple bunny with long floppy ears so tightly to her chest that it would have strangled if it had been real.

"How did it go? Was she angry?"

"No, actually it wasn't as bad as I thought it was going to be. She went really quiet, then she cried, then she hugged me and cried some more. Then we talked about practical stuff like school and getting through my NCEA." Anita gave a muffled laugh. "Dad was worse."

"Was he mad?"

"Oh yeah, but not with me. He stormed up and down the lounge ranting about rape and under-age sex. He even threatened to go to the police about Caleb till Mum pointed out that I'm sixteen so I'm not actually under age any more. He was pretty pissed about the spiked drink though and is still talking about it being technically rape."

"Well, I guess it was, in a way," I pointed out.

"Yeah, sort of but … nah... I made up my mind a while ago that I wanted to try it and Caleb was … convenient. I didn't push him away. It's as much my fault as his."

I had to stop for a second to get my head around that piece of information. Fluffy bunny Anita had been planning to have sex? Without thinking about protection? Before she even had a boyfriend? Some days I think it's not just her toys who have dacron in their heads.

"What about Caleb? Have you told him yet?"

"Yeah. Dad dragged us all over to his house last night and told him in front of his parents. It was pretty awful."

"How did they react?"

"Stunned silence. Caleb looked sick. His father offered to pay for an abortion but I told them what I thought of that idea. I am having my baby. I don't need Caleb's help. In fact, I'd rather he buggered off and left me alone."

"But he's the father. What if he wants to be involved?"

"Tough luck! Like I told them, it's my baby, my choice."

"Okay, okay, calm down. I'm not disagreeing, just asking."

"His mother suggested adopting it out – I told her where she could stick that idea too. I couldn't do that. I couldn't have a baby then give it to someone else. Imagine if you were in the mall or something and you saw your kid with someone else, I'd just want to grab it and run off. No, I'm definite. I'm having the baby and I'm keeping it, him, her, whichever."

Anita emphasised her words by thumping the defenceless toy rabbit onto her bed, then realised what she had done and gave it a cuddle, smoothing its stuffing back into place. She placed it safely on her pillow and continued.

"Anyway, speaking of babies, how's your new sister in Australia? When are you going to see her?"

"I have no idea and I care even less," I replied. "Dad keeps hassling me to go over there. He sends me emails every day or so but I'm putting him off. He's emailed me pictures – the poor little brat looks like him. I'll think about it after the show. If Severn goes straight back to France when it finishes, I'll need something to distract me till school starts again, so a trip to Oz might be a good idea. Shopping on the Gold Coast has got to be better than moping around Eastgate."

"I wish I could come too," Anita said wistfully.

"I'll bring you back some cute baby clothes," I promised.

"And a toy koala?"

"And a toy koala," I agreed.

"Severn," she said.

"He's not a koala."

"Dope! Spill! I want to hear all the gossip – ALL the gossip – every juicy detail."

I knew the juicy details she was hoping to hear, but that hadn't happened, plus there was the juicy gossip I couldn't tell her, but I filled her in as much as I could. By the time I had to leave, she was laughing and a lot more cheerful than when I had arrived. Now to find out why Mum was stressed. Onto my bike and onwards to the mall.

Mum was waiting in the food court, checking out the different flavours of muffins.

"I'll have one of those raspberry ones, plus a piece of cheesecake," I requested as I slid in beside her. "And an iced chocolate."

Our tray laden, we found ourselves a table. Mum demolished half her muffin before giving me some hint as to why she was stressing. It wasn't about Tommy.

"Your dad really wants you to go and visit," she began. "Why won't you?"

"Like I said, I will. I just wasn't going to run like a good dog when he snapped his fingers. I'll go when it suits me. I told him Easter but maybe I'll go after the show. Has he been hassling you about it?"

"A bit. Okay, a lot. He's even sent Grant an email asking him to intervene. I think he thinks we're plotting against him."

"Oh, for fu... for heaven's sake! What great plot are we supposed to be hatching?"

"The same plot he's been on at me about since we moved back here – I'm stopping him seeing his child grow up, alienating your affections, blah blah blah, generally being an uncaring human being."

"Tough shit! It's not like he didn't move on fast enough."

"Fast enough!" Mum nearly choked on her coffee. "He'd moved on before I'd moved out! That's why I moved out. He must have gone through four or five girlfriends between me and what's her name."

"Bianca," I supplied.

"What have they called the baby?" Mum asked

"Oh," I thought hard. "I can't honestly remember. He did tell me. It was some weird four-syllable thing that sounded like they had made it up. I think it started with an A, or an O."

Mum laughed. "Maybe we should buy something to send over – that might soften the blow and get him off your back."

"Yeah, we could get one of those little baby outfits with a sheep on it, or a kiwi. And maybe I'll take it over. I'll email him later and tell him I will come over when the show's finished, just for a few days. I've promised Anita I'll bring back a koala for her baby."

"For her what?"

Oops. Slip of the tongue.

"Um, yep, you heard me right. Anita's pregnant. To Caleb the violin nerd. Due in August."

"Oh my god," was all Mum could say.

CHAPTER SIXTEEN

If they made shopping an olympic sport, Mum would be at least a silver medallist. To get to the babywear, we had to pass the make-up aisle, the shoes, the women's clothes and the underwear. Or rather we had to stop at them all, try stuff on, then buy it. By the time we made it to the babywear we were both lugging several bags. We found three outfits that even I thought were cute and, as we couldn't decide which was the cutest, Mum bought all three, agreeing that I should give the one with the bunny on it to Anita. Then it was on to the supermarket to grab something quick to make for dinner.

"Final dress rehearsal tonight," Mum said as we browsed the vegetables. "Are you nervous about opening tomorrow?"

"Not any more. If Severn and the others hadn't turned up I would be freaking out, but I'm just sitting back now and letting them run it."

"Strange lot, aren't they?" Mum asked in a tome that suggested she already knew exactly why they were strange.

"How?"

"Well, there's something about those three. Where did they learn as much as they know, and get so confident, when none of them look like they're out of their teens? They look so young and they act so old. Don't you think that's a bit strange?"

I wasn't game to answer.

"David — he's fascinating. So small and so young, yet he seems to know everyone who's anyone in the business; he's worked all over the place and he takes charge like someone well used to authority. And Severn — when you look at him he looks so young and innocent, but when you talk to him it's like talking to someone more my age. Like I said, they're a strange lot. Should I, as your mother, be concerned?"

"Yeah, I guess you should," I replied. "They're strange because they're vampires."

There. I had said it. Perfectly timed so she wouldn't believe me.

"I thought so," Mum replied so seriously that I really think she wasn't kidding. "They look the part." She studied a cabbage then chose a different one. "So how come they eat garlic bread?"

"I dare you to ask them," I laughed. Later I would have to

repeat this conversation to Severn and hope he laughed too.

"The police don't seem to be getting any closer to finding young Tommy." Mum changed the subject.

"What about the cameras, surely they've got a picture."

"Apparently not. I was with Heidi this morning when the police came to tell her that the cameras were useless. She had parked in the wrong spot. The cameras were all trained either inside at the counter or outside on the pumps to catch people who drove away without paying for their petrol. Heidi had parked over by the side of the building, so one camera got her inside buying the icecream and one other got the tail end of her car but not the doors. The other two cameras got nothing at all. Heidi is a mess."

"So what are we having for tea?" I asked Mum as she put back the cabbage and hovered over the lettuces.

"Wraps," Mum made a decision. "We need lettuce, tomatoes, chicken, cheese, tortillas – and garlic bread," she added with a grin.

"To keep away the vampires?"

"Obviously not."

I had a sudden, silly thought.

"Just as well they can't make baby vampires. Imagine babies with little pointy teeth."

Mum instinctively folded her arms across her chest. "Doesn't bear thinking about."

The vampire baby conversation got us through the checkout, back to the car and home before we ran out of stupid jokes about coffin-shaped cots and other essential vampire baby accessories. My own vampires were waiting on the front step as we pulled up.

"Speaking of vampires..." Mum said.

"Shut up!" I was pretty sure that, with their super-hearing, they would have heard that. Even more sure when I saw all three heads shoot up in surprise.

"Hello, boys," Mum said sweetly. "Had a busy day? Hanging out anywhere interesting?"

I cringed.

"Not as busy as you, by the look of it," the Rev acted as if he had no idea what Mum was referring to as Mum opened the car boot to reveal all our parcels as well as my bike. "Can we give you a hand with these?"

Without waiting for a reply, the Rev and Aiden extricated all the parcels, leaving Severn to haul out my bike which we pushed into the garage before joining Mum in the kitchen where she was sorting through the parcels.

"Yours, mine, yours, mine, mine, mine, baby stuff..."

"Baby stuff?" Severn didn't actually ask that out loud but the head-down, eyebrows-lifted-over-his-glasses look said it without words.

"Baby stuff," I said firmly. "Two little outfits for my half-sister in Australia and one with a bunny on it for Anita. She is determined to have her baby and keep it."

"Go Anita," said Aiden. "Whoever Anita is."

"My best friend," I explained. "She's pregnant to a nerd from school who plays the violin."

"She'll probably make a very good mother," Mum said. "She's very caring."

"Yeah, she'll probably spoil it rotten like Heidi and it'll turn into another fat little chocolate-filled Tommy clone."

Aiden giggled.

"Sorry," he said. "I shouldn't laugh, not with him missing and all, but it's her name. I can't get my head around her being a Heidi. All I can think of are Swedish milkmaids with plaited hair and big brown cows." He paused then added, "I was surprised when I found out that she was Tommy's mother. He didn't smell like her son."

I was about to ask what he meant by that when Grant rushed in, followed by the director.

"Emergency meeting," Grant explained. "We have to work out who's replacing Tommy before we open tomorrow."

"It will have to be here in the kitchen, then," said Mum. "I need to cook chicken while we talk or nobody gets to eat."

"Chicken?" The director looked hopeful as he settled himself on a stool at the end of the bench.

"I'll cut the lettuce," I volunteered, giving in to the inevitable.

CHAPTER SEVENTEEN

An hour later we left for Mona Vale, fed, caffeinated and with a Tommy replacement organised to meet the director there. He was a year or two older than Tommy but was a more experienced actor who had done several tv advertisements, so the director was satisfied that he would take over the role with only one rehearsal before we opened to the public. Cameron and Danny had arrived before us and were hauling gear when we pulled up.

"Gee," Cameron jeered over his shoulder as he staggered past us struggling under the weight of the lighting desk. "You are here. Thought you must be having the night off."

"We'll go if you like," Aiden retorted, stepping towards Cameron and flexing his muscles in a good impression of an angry bantam rooster. Cameron faced him down, flexing his own muscles and beckoning "bring it on" with his hand. I glanced towards Severn who was already sending warning glances to the Rev. Both of them looked at Aiden, obviously expecting trouble, which didn't come.

"Now, children," Danny stepped between them and took one end of the desk. "No bickering. Let's get this stuff sorted as quickly as we can. Big night tonight. Last time to stuff up and get away with it."

Cameron listened to Danny but wasn't going to be the first to move away. Neither was Aiden who took another menacing step forwards. Cameron held his ground. I saw the Rev's mouth move so I knew he was whispering something to Aiden, who glared at him before shoving Cameron in the chest and stalking off. Cameron made a rude gesture to Aiden's departing back but I could tell he was relieved it hadn't ended in blows.

"Come on," Danny slapped him on the back. "That's enough shit for one night. Crew should work together, save the aggro for the actors. Let's get this gear sorted."

"Yeah," the Rev agreed, "Let's do it. Aiden will come back when he's calmed down."

I don't know where Aiden went but the rest of us got stuck into the usual nightly rush to set up all the equipment and make sure it was working properly. I tried to concentrate on what I was supposed to be doing but my mind kept wandering around all the baby talk I had listened to earlier in the day. Anita had really surprised me with her determination to have and keep her baby. If I'd been asked I would have thought she would have gone for the easiest option, not the hardest one. I was busily daisy-chaining speaker cables together when I remembered Aiden's odd remark about Heidi. How can someone smell like a mother? I looked around to see if he had returned and was nearby, but he was away over by the tents. Later maybe. I forced myself to concentrate on what I was doing.

Daisy chains. Who decided to use that name for joining speakers in a line, rather than one at a time back to the sound desk? I let my mind wander again. I guess it made sense. It was kind of the same as putting daisies through the stems of other daisies to make a line of them. Then you could either have a long line or join them back together in a big circle. I haven't done that since I was a little kid. I remembered Mum and I sitting on the lawn in Australia making daisy chains, or rather I would make daisy chains and Mum would watch out for the snakes she was always sure were going to bite me. Now it's vampires biting me and she seems okay with it – if she knows, which I think she does. I was so busy cabling and thinking that I wasn't watching where I was going and walked, head down, straight into a group of ladies from props and wardrobe.

"Sorry." I stepped back.

"No problem," one of the ladies replied. "You look busy."

"Yeah, lots to do." I pulled myself together and moved past them, vaguely aware that something about them wasn't quite what I expected to see. I looked back but couldn't work it out – they all looked perfectly normal. Who knows? Back to work, cables to lay.

Everyone backstage was talking about the McCormacks. No matter where I went, Tommy was the topic of conversation. Nobody believed that he had run off. Everyone had seen him throw temper tantrums to get his own way and everyone knew how much Heidi doted on him. Nobody believed that, with the promise of an icecream and probably lollies as well, he would have gone anywhere except into the shop to get the icecream quicker. Everyone thought he must have been kidnapped but nobody could think why. If it was for money, why hadn't there been a ransom demand? Angus McCormack was rich, he could pay a ransom, but everyone knew there hadn't been any mention of one. Everyone knew because three of the wardrobe ladies had been standing guard over Heidi in round-the-clock shifts and they had all the gossip from inside the McCormack house. A lot of the ladies spoke of how long Heidi had waited to have a baby and how awful it would be to lose him so young. Everyone seemed to think he was probably dead.

As I rushed around getting everything set up, something still nagged at the back of my brain. Something I should be able to see but couldn't quite get a picture of. I almost caught the thought as I crossed the wobbly bridge across the creek on my way to the smaller stage where the director was walking the new boy through his paces. Some memory flickered as I saw the Rev approach them with a radio microphone, but it was gone before I could grab hold of it. Then it was too late to worry. I heard the "five minutes to beginners" call and raced to the tower.

Severn and I settled side by side at our equipment, Severn deftly controlling the microphones and sound effects while I mixed the musicians. Everything was going smoothly, which should have warned us. Sure enough, just as Severn produced a bar of chocolate, there was a change in the sound. Severn's keen ears caught it a full minute before the stage manager's voice asked over the comms why the speakers nearest the smaller stage were no longer working. Severn replied in fluent French swear words that I didn't need a translator to understand.

"Learn that in the monastery, did you?" I laughed.

"Rev? Aiden?" Severn ignored me and spoke in a normal voice which, if you didn't know about vampires, would sound pretty strange seeing the other two were over the creek by the dressing tents. "Come back here fast!"

A few seconds later Aiden appeared at the foot of the tower, although I hadn't seen him come over the bridge. How do they do that?

"Rev's busy with radio mics," he said, not even puffing. "Riley, grab a spare cable and we'll go trouble shooting."

I left Severn in control of both desks, climbed out of the tower and set off with Aiden to find the source of the problem. We started at the speaker on the end of the daisy chain line, which seemed normal. Aiden then suggested that we work backwards down the line, pulling out each cable and replacing it with the new one to see if that fixed it. If it made no difference, we assumed the cable there was okay, put the original one back and moved further down the line. We found the problem at the third cable. As soon as we replaced it, the sound came back. Aiden and I gave each other a high five and I went back to my place in the tower.

The rest of the show wasn't too bad – for Severn and I anyway. Lighting blew a couple more bulbs, which had Danny and Cameron swearing, and from the talk over the comms I gathered props and wardrobe were having their share of last-minute problems as well. But I wasn't really listening to them. Between songs, when I had to push the right sliders, I ate chocolate and let my mind wander. Mostly my thoughts were about Severn, sitting beside me, not quite close enough to touch, which made me think how much I wanted to do just that. And have him touch me. Which led to thoughts about where. Which led to questions like "should I". Focus, Riley! Severn noticed that I wasn't concentrating and grinned as I nearly missed a song cue. Which unfocussed me again. That smile is so sexy. Focus! Think of something else. Eat more chocolate.

About halfway through my second bar of Black Forest the random bits of information that I couldn't quite grab hold of not only became clear but strung themselves together like my childhood daisy chains.

"OMG!" I heard my voice over my comms and realised I had spoken out loud.

"What's wrong? What happened? Are you all right?" Severn, Cameron and Danny's voices all came over the comms at once.

"Sorry, I'm fine. No problems," I told them quickly. Severn looked sideways at me in disbelief. I turned off the microphone on my comms unit. He saw what I did and did the same. Now we could talk but not be heard by anyone except maybe the Rev and Aiden.

"What's up?" he asked.

"I think I've figured out who took Tommy."

"Who?"

"Well, I don't know exactly who – I mean I don't know their name, but I have just had a crazy idea that might be a reason why he's missing. Oh shit! We're up to the Sheriff's entrance – song coming up. Tell you after the show."

We had packed up the gear and were ready to leave before Severn gently pulled me aside and asked about Tommy.

"Who? Why?"

I raised my hand to stop him.

"Hang onto that thought. I have a question I need to ask

Aiden before I tell anyone anything. I could be completely wrong. Aiden!"

I grabbed Aiden by the arm and pulled him off to the side of the carpark.

"Aiden, earlier you said something about Tommy not smelling like Heidi's son. What did you mean?"

"It's difficult to explain," he began. "I've got a really sensitive sense of smell – it's got some long fancy name but I can never remember it – anyway, even before I was changed, I smelled things other people couldn't. Now it's even worse, or better, depending on how you look at it. I smell things kind of how a dog does. What I meant by Tommy was that he and Heidi don't smell the same." He fumbled for a better explanation. "Um, like your family. I can tell that you are your mum's but not Grant's daughter. You and your mum don't smell exactly the same but, underneath all the other normal scents there is a basic one that smells the same. But Grant smells different. That's what fooled me with Tommy. Heidi smelled wrong."

"Thank you!" I hugged Aiden excitedly. "I think you've just answered my question." I dragged him back to the others. "Home, to my place!" I ordered. "I have a theory!"

CHAPTER EIGHTEEN

I knew I was driving Severn crazy with curiosity but, probably because of that, I purposefully took ages to make coffee and dig out biscuits before calling everyone, including Mum and Grant, into the lounge to hear my thoughts.

"I think I might know who took Tommy and why," I began.

"Who?" Mum and Grant said at once.

"Well, I don't actually know their name, but I'll tell you why first then we can work out if I am right about the who."

"Okay, why?" Grant supplied.

"Babies. It's all about babies and daisy chains."

"Of course it is," Grant gave me a look that suggested I was mental.

"Hear me out. I got this idea from the daisy chains. Things that are joined together affect each other. Like today – when the speakers stopped, it wasn't because they were broken, it was further back down the line, in a cable. So if one thing is joined to another, something that happens to an early thing might show up in a later thing. You with me?"

Everyone nodded but they all looked bewildered as if I wasn't making sense at all.

"Babies," I continued. "As you all know by now my friend Anita is having a baby. She is determined to have the baby even though others want her to get rid of it or, at least, adopt it out. It was what she said about adopting that made me think. She said that if she adopted it out, then saw it at the shops, she would want to take it back. Then, there was Danny's story about Heidi and how long she had waited to get pregnant – how everyone thought that they had given up, then she had Tommy. But she didn't just have Tommy. She quit her job and they went to live in Wanaka then came back to Christchurch with the baby. Add to that Aiden's amazing sense of smell."

Mum and Grant looked really puzzled so I explained.

"Aiden has got a sense of smell like a bloodhound." I carried on quickly before Mum got a chance to say what she was obviously thinking – of course he has, he's a vampire. "Aiden, tell Mum and Grant what you told me earlier."

"Oh, right," Aiden dithered then explained. "To me, families smell the same – underneath all the other scents. Like I told Riley, she smells like you," he pointed to Mum, "but not like you," he pointed to Grant, "so I knew that you weren't her actual father. Anyway, Heidi doesn't smell like Tommy."

"So!" I wound up my argument. "I think that Heidi isn't Tommy's real mother. I think they hid out in Wanaka so no-one would notice that she wasn't actually pregnant and they bought a baby off someone else. And I think that his real mother has turned up and taken him away."

I wasn't sure what reaction I was expecting from my announcement but I didn't expect what I got – complete silence. For at least a minute. Then heads began to nod and mumbles of agreement grew into words.

"That's an interesting theory," Grant said at last. "But where did this mystery mother appear from and how come she got him away from the car without him screaming his head off? I mean, he wouldn't know she was his mother – I bet, if it's true, he won't even know he's not Heidi's – so he wouldn't just waltz off with some complete stranger who says she's his mum when he knows his mum is inside buying him an icecream. It doesn't make sense."

"What if he did know her?" I asked. "Even if he didn't know she was his mother. What if he thought she was a friend?"

"But then Heidi would know her and surely she wouldn't have her around?"

"She might," Mum answered. "Some people have arrangements with natural mothers where they can see the children and some kids grow up thinking that their natural mother is their aunt or cousin."

"Or she's been hanging around behind Heidi's back," I added.

"Are you thinking of someone in particular?" Mum realised I had another part to my theory.

"Yep. That strange woman who was around the show all through rehearsals. The one in the striped skirt who looked like a reject from a gipsy fair."

"I thought she was part of the wardrobe department," Mum said.

"So did I, but let's face it, did any of you ever see her anywhere near the dressing tents? Or with a costume in her hands? The only place I have ever seen her is either talking to Tommy behind the little stage, or sitting on the edge of the green under a tree, watching him on stage."

"I'll agree with that," the Rev added. "I tried to speak to her once, asked her what department she was with, and she didn't answer, just mumbled something about being busy and dashed off as fast as she could. Strange woman."

"If your theory is right," asked Grant, "what do we do about it? Should we go to the police?"

"And tell them what?" the Rev enquired. "It's a random theory – okay it's quite a good theory, but it's still only a theory. The police are just going to think Riley is a nut case, thank you politely and push you out the door as quickly as possible. It's not like we have any evidence to back it up."

"He's right," I agreed. "And, anyway, after the Tasha thing I'd rather not go anywhere near the police if I don't have to."

Severn nodded in agreement.

"We could get some evidence," Mum suggested. "We could talk to Heidi."

"And ask her outright if Tommy's not hers?" Grant was incredulous.

"Exactly," Mum replied. "That's exactly what I need to do. Riley, you come with me and we will go and talk to Heidi. Right now."

"Um, it's nearly midnight," I pointed out.

"So? If Tommy is in danger, every minute counts."

"But if my theory is right, he's not in any danger so another night won't make any difference. And if he is in danger, then my theory is wrong anyway, so either way, visiting Heidi can wait until tomorrow."

"Tomorrow is probably better," Grant agreed. "Heidi's probably doped up with sedatives and asleep by now. Let's go to bed, get a good night's sleep, then we can ring them in the morning and let them know we are coming over. I'll ring work and tell them I won't be in till later and come with you – I can talk to Angus while you two are interrogating Heidi."

"I guess you're right," Mum said. "Tomorrow will do. I am tired." She stood up. "Good night all. Oh, I hope Tommy's having a good night. I hope he is with someone who cares about him and not somewhere horrible, all scared and alone."

Grant led the way out the door but Mum turned back to say enigmatically, "Good night, boys. Enjoy the rest of the night, doing … whatever your sort do… in the night."

Three sets of eyes watched her leave then turned on me.

"What did she mean by that?" the Rev asked, his voice soft but tinged with menace.

"I think she knows," I answered honestly. "My mother is freaky sometimes. She knows things she shouldn't. Like, if she meets Anita she'll know just by being beside her for a few minutes what sex the baby will be – and she'll be right. She knows who's on the phone before she picks it up."

"Yes, she does," Severn backed me up. "Last time, I was sure she knew what I was – she was always humming the "Lost Boys" theme music and quoting that line from the movie about 'all the damn vampires'."

"She gets it from her grandmother," I explained. "Great-grandma was a psychic – she read tarot cards and tea leaves. Grandma didn't want to know about it but Mum used to stay with Great-grandma and I think she learned a lot more than she lets on."

"Can you do it too?" Aiden asked.

"No. I'm as psychic as a brick. I think it must jump every second generation. If I ever have a girl she might have it. But don't under-estimate Mum. I'm sure she's known about you guys from the beginning. She did ask me some odd questions when we were out shopping and I admit that, to see her reaction, I said sure, you guys were odd because you were all vampires."

"And her reaction was...?" Severn's tone was half amused, half scathing.

"Her reaction was, of course they are. No, hang on, her actual words were 'they look the part'."

Like a bad movie, all three looked each other and themselves up and down then shook their heads in disbelief.

"So what do we do now? Tell everyone? Take our shirts off at opening night and fly over Mona Vale?" Severn showed no amusement now.

"Don't be stupid! Mum isn't going to tell anyone. She doesn't go around telling everyone that she's a psychic witch who can predict things, so she's not likely to tell anyone that her daughter's going out with a vampire, is she? Who'd believe her anyway? It's not the sort of conversation you have with the ladies backstage – nice boy your daughter's going out with – oh yes, he's a vampire, you know."

"So what should we do?" the Rev asked.

"Nothing. Ignore her silly jokes – or fire your own joke back at her. Just don't admit it or give her any actual proof – like, leave your shirts on and don't show your wings - and don't bite anyone."

"Okay, so, what are we going to do right now? How are we going to spend the rest of the night?"

"Doing whatever 'our sort' do," Severn laughed.

'I don't know about 'your sort'," I laughed back, "but 'my sort' is going to bed – to sleep!" I added quickly in answer to Severn's hopefully raised eyebrow.

"In that case," the Rev finished, "our sort will leave you and disappear quietly into the night."

"I'm hungry," I heard Aiden say as they left. I didn't want to think what kind of hunger he was talking about.

CHAPTER NINETEEN

Over breakfast Mum and I rehearsed our approach to Heidi as if it were a show. Mum tried out various different ways of asking "did you buy your baby" till we found the right words and a delivery style that sounded caring and considerate. Mum sure can act!

The only reference she made to vampires was to ask where the boys were heading after they left our place. I was relieved that I could answer honestly that I didn't know. I could imagine – I'd seen it before – but if I didn't think too hard I could ignore all the nagging doubts. I did not want to know that my boyfriend was sucking the blood out of someone he picked up in a downtown nightclub and shared with his mates.

By ten o'clock we had rehearsed our lines enough and plucked up enough courage to set out on our mission; Grant driving, Mum fretting, me clutching a printout of the photo I had emailed Severn - the one that had the skirt woman caught on my cell phone camera while I had been photographing the musicians paddling in the lake. At the McCormacks' house, it was pretty obvious that Heidi was almost at breaking point. Instead of the immaculate, high-fashion woman who strutted around like royalty, she was a mess – hair straggly and unbrushed, eyes red, face puffy. She slouched in an armchair, curled up under a blanket. I wasn't sure she even knew we were there. Mr McCormack, in contrast, seemed to be much more in control. He was dressed tidily in what Grant would describe as 'casual business' clothes – neat trousers and a shirt without a tie. He was the one who greeted us at the door, showed us through to Heidi and offered us tea or coffee, which we refused, before allowing Grant to lead him away so we could speak to Heidi alone.

Mum started gently, holding Heidi's hand while encouraging her to answer basic questions. It took a while to get her attention through all the sedation, but Mum continued to talk quietly to her and gradually she began to respond.

"I miss him so much," she wailed through a wall of tears, "He's my whole life. I just want him back. I feel so helpless sitting here waiting. I want to be out there looking. The police say I am better off here by the phone but it's driving me crazy. Oh Tommy! Where are you?"

Mum handed her another pile of tissues from the box next to her chair and patted her hand, calming her with soothing words. At first she got Heidi talking about Tommy at school, his favourite subjects, his hobbies, how he was enjoying being in the show. Her plan worked. Heidi started hesitantly, recounting her pride in a certificate Tommy had won for maths and how he sang a song at the final school assembly last year, then she warmed up to her favourite subject and soon we knew way more about Tommy than we remotely cared about.

Mum continued to nod and smile, reminding me of those wobbly-head dogs some people have in the back window of their cars. Doing some of her best acting in the role of concerned hand-holding friend, Mum coaxed Heidi backwards through Tommy's life. I sat in the background, keeping completely quiet and trying not to fidget so I didn't break the spell Mum was weaving. She would make a good hypnotist. Maybe she is a good hypnotist. Maybe she has been subliminally programming me for years. Is that why I don't mind doing the ironing? No point asking her though – she'll just deny it, then reprogram me with something else. Something worse – like cleaning the windows. Concentrate, Riley! And sit still! No, your nose is not itchy. It does not need scratching! I tuned back in to hear Heidi relating some story about Tommy with a favourite rattle, so I guessed we must be close to the moment of truth. I suddenly imagined Mum as a vampire, ready to open her mouth and sink her pointy teeth into Heidi's neck, sucking the truth out of her. I really needed to move – why had I chosen the most uncomfortable chair in the room?

Mum pounced.

"Heidi," she began softly, patting Heidi's hand like she was a good puppy. "I need to ask you something difficult. I'm not sure if it's true or not and I know you won't want to talk about, but it could be very, very important. Will you promise to answer me honestly if it helps us find Tommy?"

Heidi nodded soundless agreement.

"When Tommy was born," Mum paused slightly then continued still in a gentle, soothing tone like a lullaby, "it wasn't you, was it? Did someone else give birth to Tommy? Did she give him to you?"

"No, no, he's mine, she …" Heidi struggled, confused, then sank back into her chair defeated, pulling the rug higher around her chin. "Yes," she admitted in a voice so tiny we could barely hear her. "Yes, you're right. How did you know? Nobody knows."

"Riley guessed," Mum answered. "She thinks that might be where he is – with his real mother."

"He wouldn't do that." Heidi's voice gained some of its normal strength. "He doesn't know anything about her."

"No, but she knows about him," I joined in. "I think she's taken him. Which is good for Tommy as there is no way she is going to hurt him. But we need to figure out who she is and where she is so we can get him back. What's her name?"

Mum put out a hand to stop me talking

"Slow down," she said. "Riley, can you please go and get Grant and Angus. I think they need to be here before we go any further. Heidi, I'm going to make us a nice cup of tea, then we'll talk some more. Okay?"

"I'll make the tea," I volunteered. I didn't think leaving Heidi alone was a good idea. Mum smiled her thanks.

I found Grant and Angus in the kitchen, already loading mugs of tea onto a tray. I wondered if they had been listening. With Grant holding the tray before him like a sacrificial offering, we returned to the lounge, Grant placing the tray reverentially on a delicate coffee table and handing Heidi a mug colourfully decorated with large red cats. Angus moved to what was obviously his favourite chair, but sat precariously on its edge as if he expected to leap up at any moment. Mum raised her eyebrows to Grant in a silent question.

"I've had a chat with Angus," Grant began. "He has confirmed Riley's guess. And Heidi?"

Mum nodded. "Yes, Heidi has told us that Tommy was born to someone else." She turned to Angus. "I presume, though, that he wasn't legally adopted - through the Social Welfare. I'm guessing the birth was kept quiet and you two just registered him as yours?"

Heidi and Angus both nodded dumbly in reply.

"She stayed with us in Wanaka," Angus explained. "Our house there has a little guest house attached, so she stayed there. It's in a quiet part of the town, further around the lake, so nobody overlooks it. It was easy to stay out of the way. It was a home birth. We managed it ourselves. Then we paid her off and she left."

"You paid her off?" I could tell by his tone that Grant was trying to remain calm but he was actually quite revolted by

Angus's casual explanation of buying a baby. I was pretty revolted as well. I'm not a big fan of babies but babies are not the same as puppies, buying them was just wrong.

"Yes," Angus replied. "It was all agreed long before she gave birth. We paid her a weekly allowance while she was pregnant, to make up for her lost wages, a substantial down-payment when we made our agreement, a rather large sum on the birth and I agreed to make regular payments every year for ten years to ensure she kept her mouth shut and stayed away."

"How did you find her in the first place?" Mum asked, intrigued.

"She worked in the cake shop beside the shop I worked in," Heidi answered. "I found her out the back one day, in tears as she had just found out that she was pregnant. She wasn't married and came from a very religious family, so she was looking for a way out. I was desperate for a baby, so I came up with the plan and she agreed. She told her parents that she had a job in Wanaka as our housekeeper and off we went."

"And it's worked very well," added Angus haughtily. "Heidi has her baby, Tommy has the best of everything and we haven't heard from her since she walked out our door. But you clearly think otherwise. Why do you think she has returned?"

"I think you've already given us the answer to that," I said.

"I have?"

"Yes. The money. You said that you had an agreement to pay her something every year for ten years. Why ten?"

Angus shrugged. "It seemed sensible at the time. Ten years would give us all time to get on with our lives – particularly her. It would give her enough time to get back on her feet, but not leave us in debt to her for ever."

"Absolutely," I thought but didn't say out loud, "can't possibly take someone's baby and be in debt to them." Angus McCormack was a selfish tosser.

"Tommy's ten now, isn't he?" I asked, even though I knew the answer. "You've made your last payment to her?"

"Yes, I made the final payment to her on Tommy's birthday back in October."

"There's your answer then," I said triumphantly. "As long as your money was coming in, she's kept her side of the bargain and stayed away. Now it's stopped she's come back to take him back."

"That wasn't the deal!" Heidi straightened in anger. "He

wasn't on loan!"

"Maybe she thought he was. Maybe she regretted giving him up and has been waiting for the right time. Who knows? We won't know why till we find her. So back to the question I asked ages ago – what's her name?"

"Sally. Sally Murchison," Heidi answered, sinking back into the chair and pulling the rug tighter.

"Is this her?" I pulled the photo of the flouncy skirt lady from my pocket and passed it to Heidi, who shook her head.

"I don't know." She handed the photo to Angus. "It's been so long. What do you think?"

"Could be," he nodded. "She's changed a lot, if it is. Got a lot older."

"Haven't we all," Grant said.

"I meant she's aged badly. If it is her, she looks older than she is. I've seen that woman hanging around the show – I must admit I didn't recognise her."

"Neither did I," Heidi agreed. "But I never saw her close up. She was always over by the edge of the lake and I'm usually backstage, on stage or in the tent."

"We all thought she was with wardrobe," Mum added.

"I saw her several times talking to Tommy," I said. "That's what made me think it might be her. She hasn't been around since he disappeared."

"She was talking to Tommy?" Heidi sat forwards again, angry at the information.

"Yes. She keep getting in my road, fiddling with his microphone. I was really rude to her the other day."

"So what do we do now?" Grant asked. "Should we tell the police and get them out looking for her?"

"No!" the McCormacks said at once.

"No," Angus replied, calmer. "That would not be the best idea. Let's face it, what we did back then wasn't exactly legal. We didn't go through a formal adoption, so we can hardly go to the police now and tell them the truth. Even if we got Tommy back, the authorities would take him away and none of us would see him again. Not to mention, Heidi and I might go to prison. Or worse – the authorities might give him to her! So no, we will not tell the police. They're doing a good job with tracking dogs and pictures in the paper – we'll just let them get on with their job. We have to find another way to find Sally Murchison."

Mum had an idea. "If she's been hanging around the show, someone must have talked to her. We can ask them all tonight, pass her picture around, see if anyone knows anything about her."

Grant gulped down the last of his tea.

"Better idea," he exclaimed, springing from his chair. "We don't have to wait till tonight. Riley – you've got that photo on the computer?" I nodded. "Right, let's get home and I'll email it out to the cast and crew list. We might get a reply before tonight." He turned to Heidi. "Don't worry, we'll find Tommy." Then to Angus. "Start thinking. Any information you've got on her at all."

He strode out the door determinedly, Mum and I following like obedient sheep. Obedient but rapidly-thinking sheep.

CHAPTER TWENTY

To: robinhoodcastandcrewlist
From: grantathome
Subject: tommy
attached: idiotsinlake.jpg
To all cast and crew – we need your help. Please find attached a photo of some of you by the lake. Take a good look at the woman in the photo. We think she may be connected to Tommy's disappearance and we need to find out who she is. If any of you have spoken to her, or have any clues to her identity at all, please email me back asap. Any information is good. We think her name is Sally – or she may be calling herself something different. Has she mentioned a favourite shop? Have you seen her eating something out of a bag with an identifiable label? Does she live near Mona Vale? Anything, no matter how trivial, please let me know. Thanks, Grant.

The useful answers were slow in coming. The first replies were all just saying sorry, never spoke to her. It wasn't looking too good. Mum consoled us while we waited anxiously by suggesting that I text the vampires – well, she called them the boys, not the vampires – and get them to bring pizza, which they did. We sat, we ate, we waited, we threw ideas around, we ate more. It was about two hours before the first useful answer arrived.

To: grantathome
From: marganddave
Subject: RE tommy
Hi Grant.
I might have something useful. I think she lives over near Beckenham. It was that day the council had Barrington Street closed for major road works and a few of us got held up in the detour. We were all bitching about how long it took us to get to Mona Vale and she joined in, saying how she had gone "back" to Colombo Street and risked biking down Moorhouse and around the bottom of the park. If she went "back" to Colombo then she must have come from around there to start with, which makes me think she lives in Beckenham or nearby. Cheers, Marg (the props lady who handles your sword haha)

"Does she now?" Mum laughed at the sign-off.

"Every night," Grant grinned. "Seriously, though, that's huge – the information, not the sword, Susan get your mind out of the gutter! That means she lives close to the McCormacks. Tommy might be just around the corner from them."

'That makes sense," the Rev broke in. "If she's been planning this for a while, then she would need somewhere close by to take him. If she only has a bike then she's going to know she wouldn't have time to cycle with him on the back right across town before the alarm went up. Or if she's been watching their house and was waiting for a chance to lure him away, she'd need to get him out of sight fast. Either way, if it was me, somewhere close would be my choice."

"That's good, isn't it?" Aiden asked.

You'd think!" Grant replied. "But I doubt she's going to have a big arrow in the window saying 'here I am'. It might have made the haystack a bit smaller, but it's still a bloody big one for the size of the needle we're hunting for."

"Lighten up!" I growled. "It's gone from a whole city to a few blocks. I have an idea. Let's drive around the area and check out the corner dairies, see if anyone recognises her photo. If there's one she goes to regularly, it might narrow the area even more."

The Rev jumped to his feet. "Let's do it! Come on guys!" Severn, Aiden and I moved as one, following the Rev out the door to their car.

"We'll stay here and man the fort," Mum called after us.

"I'll text you," I called back before piling into the back seat beside Severn, who put his arm around me and pulled me close. Such a shame I had to pull away and click in my seatbelt.

I navigated and Aiden drove, racing down Aldwins Road, bouncing over the railway lines, racing an orange light through the corner into Brougham Street, jumping lanes then a hard left and we were through Burlington and into Milton Street. Aiden pulled up outside a line of little shops on the corner of Colombo Street.

"Should we start here?" he asked.

I thought for a bit.

"No, McCormack's house is down in Fisher Ave. We should start with the shops closer to there."

"Okay, where do I go?"

"Left, then down further – drive, I'll tell you where to stop"

We cruised slowly down Colombo Street, me briefly wondering if this was what it felt like to be a boy racer, then wondering if Cameron did this on the Friday nights when he wasn't working a show, then wondering if I could ride with him one night to find out what it was like, then feeling guilty because I shouldn't be thinking of Cameron with Severn beside me, his hand holding mine.

"What about that shop?" the Rev's voice brought me back to reality. He was pointing at a tiny shop front with a large, hand-painted sign announcing organic vegetables and free-range eggs.

"Yes!" I exclaimed. "That's exactly the sort of place she would shop. It's worth a try."

Aiden found a parking space and I undid my seatbelt.

"You guys stay here," I said. "You don't look like health food types."

"I'll come," said Severn. "Two sets of eyes, ears, you know…"

That turned out to be a good decision. We went into the shop separately, I went first with Severn a few steps behind so we looked like two independent customers. Severn moved behind a display stand and pretended to study bottles of vitamins. I showed the two shop assistants the photo and asked if the woman in it shopped there. They both said no but something in the way they looked at each other made me not believe them. I said thanks and as I turned to walk away I heard one of them whisper, but couldn't make out what she said. I knew Severn would have heard every word.

"What did they whisper?" I asked as we climbed back into the car.

"Her exact words were 'isn't she the one who comes in on Thursdays to buy eggs? She lives around the corner in that cute little cottage just along from the church'."

"Brilliant!" I kissed him. "Aiden, drive us around the corner. Let's find us a cute little cottage."

It was pretty obvious. Among all the impressive old villas with huge, neat gardens there was a tiny little cottage painted a delicate shade of blue with a tiny garden overflowing with randomly planted wild flowers. It had to be the place. We pulled past, turned the car around and parked across the road, then gave each other high fives.

It was also too good to be true. Severn decided to check it out, quickly deciding on the cover story of being a Jehovah's Witness. Aiden offered to go along but I reminded him that she would know him by sight while she may not recognise Severn who was usually out of sight on the tower, not running around the ground with microphones in his hand. Severn, dressed in his usual black with his geeky, tortoiseshell-rimmed glasses looked enough like a religious caller to fake it, even with his ultra-short haircut. He set off across the road.

We watched from the safety of the car as he strode confidently up the path and knocked on the door. Nothing happened. He knocked again. Still nothing. We saw him look around then peer in one of the windows. He looked back at the car then set off around the side of the house, presumably looking for a back door. We waited. A few minutes later he returned, looking over at us and shrugging to indicate confusion. I saw his lips move and the Rev translated.

"He says it looks empty."

"Doesn't mean Tommy's not in there," I answered.

"He says he can't hear him," the Rev said. I wasn't surprised that Severn had heard me. "Hey, Severn," the Rev continued, "there's a neighbour coming your way."

Severn changed direction, walked over to the fence dividing the cottage from the villa next door and spoke to an elderly man holding a garden rake. Again the Rev translated for me.

"The old guy is asking Severn if he's looking for the woman who lived there. Sev says yes and is asking if she wears long striped skirts like a gipsy. Old guy says yes she does but Sev is too late, she moved out yesterday! Damn it! He doesn't know where she went. Sev's asking if there was a boy with her. Old guy says no, he hadn't seen one but his wife thought she heard a child yelling a couple of days ago. They talked about whether it came from her place but decided it was probably from the house behind them. "

The man returned to his gardening and Severn retraced his way down the path. He paused at the gate, pulled something out of the letterbox and sprinted over the road to the car.

"I gathered you heard all that," he said as he climbed in.

"Yes," the Rev replied, "And I passed it on to Riley."

I fleetingly wondered how long it would be before I could hear as well as they could, then focused on the envelope Severn was opening.

"What have you got there?" I asked.

"A solution, maybe," he replied.

I read the logo on the piece of paper as he unfolded it. "It's a power bill."

"Exactly. Let's go back to your place, I need a computer."

CHAPTER TWENTY ONE

Back at our place, Severn was first in the door and racing into Grant's office before the rest of us were out of the car. By the time we caught up with him he was in front of the computer, mumbling to himself and feverishly typing instructions.

"Coffee?" I asked.

"Mmm," was the only reply I got but I took that to mean yes and headed back to the kitchen to join the others, make coffee and to fill Mum and Grant in on what was happening.

"So what's Severn doing?" Mum asked.

I was just about to say that I didn't know when he walked in, looking frustrated. He flung himself into a chair, running his hands through his short hair.

"Damn!" he swore. ""Sorry, Grant, no offence, but your computer sucks big time. I need a faster one."

"What are you trying to do?" Grant asked.

"Hack the power company," Severn replied.

"Hack the power company?" Grant sounded secretly impressed. "You can do that?"

"Yeah, I should be able to – if I had a faster computer. I figure that if she had moved house, then she had to let the power company know so they could cut off the power at the cottage and turn it on wherever she moved to. So, all I have to do is burrow into the power company's site and get her new address. It should be easy!"

"In that case, come with me," Grant grabbed his car keys. "Let's go to my work and use the computer there. Ultra-fast broadband and the computers were all upgraded two months ago."

"Awesome," Severn smiled in relief. "Let's go."

They left and the rest of us sat, drinking coffee, feeling helpless and waiting. I could tell that the stress was getting to Mum as she decided to bake – her second-favourite stress relief if she couldn't go shopping. She had a batch of chocolate biscuits in the oven and a cake half mixed by the time Severn and Grant returned, Severn grinning from ear to ear and waving two pieces of paper.

"Got her!" He sat down, spreading the papers on the table in front of him. One of them was the power bill he had taken from the letterbox of the blue cottage, the other a picture of the front of a house – it looked like a street view from a google map. "Once I was into the power company's site it was easy to follow her as her account number stays the same, it just got changed to a different address." Severn looked smug.

"So where is she?" Mum and I asked at once.

"Westmorland, wherever that is," Severn replied.

"It's up the very top of the hills," Mum supplied. "Big houses, lots of money. Have you got an actual street number?"

Severn pushed the picture into the centre of the table.

"She's here. In Ravensdale Rise. I googled it and printed out the picture so we know what we're looking for."

"Did you print out the aerial view?" the Rev asked, then when Mum looked at him strangely he added quickly, "It would be handy to have an idea of the whole area – for planning." Mum frowned suspiciously. The Rev countered her frown with a disarming smile. "We have to plan this like a military exercise," he continued. "Now that we have an address we have to reconnoitre, then plan. Aiden, you're driving. Riley, you're navigating. Let's go check this place out."

The drive around the foot of the Cashmere Hills made me think Aiden would make a good boy racer and could probably take out Cameron if he had a decent car and not the cheap rental we were in. I was holding my breath as Aiden cut corners, drove through orange lights and generally scared the hell out of me. When Severn squeezed my hand I realised I had been gripping his so tightly that, if he had been a human and not a vampire, his blood would have stopped flowing. Forcing myself to breathe normally, I warned Aiden that the turning to the suburb of Westmorland was approaching on the left, then grabbed hold of the door handle as he swung the car around the corner without slowing down. Whatever natural abilities got enhanced when people became vampires, driving wasn't one of them. Or maybe it was. Maybe Aiden wasn't a terrible driver – maybe it was vampire-enhanced skills that let him slide around corners without crashing or turning the car over. Whichever, it was too scary to look as we sped around the corners. I closed my eyes and squeezed Severn's hand as tightly as I could. He laughed and squeezed back.

Aiden's question of "where to?" forced me to open my eyes again so I could direct him around the Westmorland streets till we reached the higher parts of Ravensdale Rise. As the numbers on the letterboxes got closer to our destination, Aiden slowed down. By the time we passed the house we were cruising at a sedate pace, slow enough for us to look in but not so slow that anyone seeing us would get suspicious. There was no sign of life but the Rev spotted a woman's bicycle propped against the house near the front door.

"What next?" Aiden asked.

"Carry on to the end of the street," I suggested. "We'll run out of road soon, so we can turn around and cruise back past."

"Turn around, come back and park a few houses away," Severn said. "I'll go for a walk past, see what I can spot."

As we approached the end of the street, the houses ended, replaced by paddocks of grazing horses, then the road stopped. Aiden turned the car around and drove back down the hill, stopping five houses away from our target.

"You drive on past and park further down the road," Severn instructed. "I'll walk past and meet you down the road." He climbed out and Aiden pulled out, drove around the next bend and parked again to wait for Severn's return. It didn't take long. A few minutes later he climbed back into the car, smiling.

"Find something?" the Rev asked.

"Yes, she's there. I spoke to her."

"You what?" I gasped.

"I went to the front door," Severn laughed. "Told her I was from the power company and was checking that her connection had been completed satisfactorily. She bought it, confirmed her name and even thanked me for caring."

"What about Tommy?" I asked.

"I didn't see him but I could hear someone else in the house walking about in an upstairs room."

"What do we do now?"

"Let's drive back to your place," the Rev suggested. "We've got a show to do in another couple of hours and we need to plan. I need to think. I've got a vague idea but I need to think it out some more. Need coffee!"

I laughed out loud.

"What's so funny?" the Rev queried in a tone that suggested he was insulted.

"You guys. I mean, vampires are supposed to say stuff like 'I vant to drink your blood'," I said in my best imitation of a bad Germanic vampire accent, "not 'I vant to drink some coffee'."

"Okay," Severn laughed, turning in his seat to pull me towards him, "I vant to drink your blood." He lowered his lips to my neck kissing then nibbling gently.

I laughed but didn't push him away. It felt good.

In the rear-vison mirror I saw Aiden lick his lips.

CHAPTER TWENTY TWO

Back at home Severn related his story to Mum and Grant and Grant promptly grabbed the phone to call the McCormacks, Grant putting Angus on speakerphone so we could all talk. Severn told his tale for the third time and Angus was delighted. We heard him tell Heidi the good news and I'm sure the neighbours heard her scream with joy. Angus asked for the address so he could drive straight there and reclaim Tommy but the Rev waved a hand to stop Grant passing on the information.

"Not a good idea," he said quietly.

"Why not?" demanded Angus. "Have you got a better one? Are we supposed to sit here and do nothing?"

"Yes and yes," the Rev replied calmly. "Yes, I have a better idea and yes I want you to sit there and do nothing."

"You can't tell me what to do!" Angus started to get belligerent. "He's my son! You have to give me the address! Right now!" His temper increased to where he was beginning to shout. "You have no right to keep this from me! Who do you think you are?"

The Rev countered his anger with quiet calm. "I am the man with a good plan to get your son back."

"Man!" Angus retorted scathingly. "You lot are not men, you're boys. Teenage boys! You may be good at theatre lighting but what the hell do you know about anything else? What's so special about your plan then? What's so special about you, for heaven's sake?"

"If only you knew," I thought, catching a tiny hint of a smirk from Severn that showed he was thinking exactly the same thing.

"My plan is better than yours because it is a plan, thought through carefully, not running off at the mouth in anger." The Rev remained calm in the face of McCormack's fury, studiously ignoring the dig about their supposed age. McCormack would have a fit if he found out that the Rev was born in the early 1300s and was nearly seven hundred years old. He hadn't been a boy for a very long time. Through those long centuries the Rev had certainly learnt some people-handling skills. Faced with an opponent who refused to argue back, Angus McCormack calmed down as quickly as he had flared up.

"What is this grand plan then?" he asked in a far more

moderate tone.

"From your point of view, it's simple," the Rev replied. "You wait at home with Mrs McCormack, keep each other calm and do nothing. Just trust me, trust me, and I guarantee that by tomorrow Tommy will be returned to you. If you let me do it my way. Can you do that?"

"Please bring him back safely," Heidi's voice came through the phone. Although we couldn't see her, I could imagine her clinging to her husband as she continued. "We'll do whatever you think best. Just bring him back to us."

"I promise I will," the Rev said quietly. "I promise I will."

Grant turned off the phone's speaker and continued to speak to Mr McCormack while the rest of us sat staring at the Rev, waiting for him to explain. He didn't.

"Come on, guys, we've got a show to do," he said instead. "Riley, get your blacks on fast, then we'll get junk food on the way to Mona Vale. I'll explain my grand plan after we've got the show packed in. Move it!"

We moved. I raced to my room, changed rapidly out of my blue jeans into my stage backs then raced back to pile into the car. Questions were thrown at the Rev from the minute Aiden started the engine.

"Come on, then, what's this plan?" Aiden asked as he reversed out of our driveway.

The Rev didn't so much laugh as chortle and splutter. "Actually I haven't got one."

"What?" Aiden turned to look at the Rev and almost swerved the car into the gutter. He wrenched the steering wheel to straighten the car and glared at the Rev. "What do you mean you haven't got one? You told McCormack you had a, what was it, a grand plan. Not just an ordinary plan - a grand one, and now you're saying that was bullshit and you haven't got any plan at all?"

"Correct," the Rev answered in the same calm voice he had used on McCormack.

"So why did you tell him you had a plan?"

"First off, he called it a 'grand' plan, I didn't. I just didn't correct him. And I let him think I had one to shut him up and to stop him rushing off up the hill, which would have done no good at all."

"How do you know that?" I asked. "Why couldn't he have

just driven up there, knocked on the door and demanded Tommy back."

The Rev sighed as if I was a complete idiot. "Because she would have seen him coming and either not answered the door, or escaped out the back, or, I don't know, whatever, it would not have ended up well. No, we need to think of something that will get the kid back without causing a scene and somehow get it through her head not to go near him again. I just don't actually know what that plan is – yet. So, while we set the show up, you guys can think of one."

"We can think of one?" Aiden was not impressed. "And just what are you going to do, Oh Great Lord and Master?"

"Glad to hear you recognise my leadership," the Rev said sweetly. "I'm going to rig some microphones and filter all your weirder suggestions until something sensible emerges."

"Huh!" was Aiden's only reply. Severn smothered a giggle.

"Why don't we just tip off the police and let them get him back?" I asked innocently.

That received an even bigger sigh and an even more scathing glare from the Rev.

"Because then she would tell the police about the illegal adoption and the whole thing would turn into an even bigger disaster than it is already," he explained with false patience. "We want to get Tommy home, not taken away by the social workers."

That effectively killed the conversation which left the rest of the drive to Mona Vale a silent affair, each of us trying and failing to come up with a plan. Once we got to the show little Tommy's fate was temporarily forgotten as we got stuck into our daily ritual of carrying gear and running out cables.

It was a strange opening night – it felt more like a second night. Instead of a feeling of excitement with lots of energy, cast and crew were all pre-occupied with speculation about Tommy. Even though the stage manager exhorted everyone to be on top form, the acting had a weird flat quality and the singing was flatter. Except Mum's of course – she couldn't sing flat if she tried. The only excitement was backstage where Grant's email had everyone talking. It seemed that just about everybody in the cast and crew had noticed the woman in the flouncy skirt but hardly anybody had actually talked to her. The musicians remembered her hanging around watching them from the trees but the bass player was the only one of them who had spoken to her, although it was only a muttered "lovely day" greeting as he walked past her on his way to the stage. The props ladies had talked to her the most. Marg, the lady who handled Grant's sword, was a friendly person who chatted to everyone, so it was only natural that she would say hello to our suspect every day. During the rehearsals Marg had made a point of talking to her any time there was a long break for meals, even offering some of her home-made baking. That had led to conversations about healthy food, free-range eggs, sustainable living and other subjects that fitted in well with our finding of the local health food shop where she was known.

"I asked her once if she had any children," Marg had related before the show to an enthusiastic audience which included Mum and me. "She went quiet, sounded very sad and said yes she did – she had a son but he wasn't living with her at the moment. I assumed that she had split up from her husband and that he was with him. Then she brightened up and said that, if all went well, he would be coming back to live with her again soon and that she had plans to move to the North Island and live in the Coromandel with, how did she put it," Marg paused to think of the right words then continued, "other people who thought about life the way she did."

"That does kind of suggest that she'd been planning this for quite a while," Mum said, more to me than to the rest of the group.

"But it doesn't make sense," Marg answered her. "Why Tommy? If she had a child of her own, why would she kidnap Tommy? That's what I don't get."

Remembering quickly that we were the only ones who knew the truth about Tommy's parentage and realising that we had to keep the secret, Mum went into that acting/telling lies thing that she was getting rather too good at.

"Perhaps…" I could almost hear her brain racing. "Perhaps she was hoping to get her own child back, then something went wrong and she snapped and grabbed Tommy instead."

"That's probably what happened," I backed Mum up. "Or maybe there never was a child of her own – maybe she made that up."

"Or maybe she had one who died young and she never recovered," Mum tried a different possibility.

"Yes, yes," Marg nodded her agreement to all our suggestions. "Whatever has happened, she's obviously not right in the head any more. I hope the police find her soon and get Tommy back safely."

I nodded, not daring to speak in case I let slip that the police hadn't been told. Mum took up the slack, carefully skirting the truth.

"I'm sure Angus has been keeping in close contact with the police. We were over there this morning and by the time we left, they were both feeling more hopeful of a speedy end to this horrible ordeal. In the meantime," she sensibly ended the conversation, "Riley, we'd better move. Things to do, show must go on and all that."

CHAPTER TWENTY THREE

I guess the audience didn't notice the lack of energy in the show, or the flat singing, or maybe the audience was so full of the cast's families and supporters they wouldn't care how bad it was. Whatever, at the end of the show they clapped and clapped until the cast had taken three extra curtain calls. Finally it was all over except for the crew's usual task of packing everything up again into the container; a task hampered by the milling crowds who were hanging around waiting to congratulate their friends and family members. I got really sick of saying "excuse me" to people who stood over or on the cables I was trying to coil and by only half way through the task I was biting my tongue so I didn't just yell "get the f*** off my cable, you moron." Aiden wasn't as controlled. I heard him shout something very similar but with a few extra swear words as he struggled to single-handedly dismantle a bank of lights.

"Morons!" I muttered to him as we passed along the track to the container.

"Yep," he replied. "Especially that guy over there with your boy racer."

I looked over where he was pointing, to see Cameron trying to fend off unhelpful help from a well-meaning but obviously useless friend.

"He is not 'my' boy racer," I retorted indignantly.

"Ooh, sorry," Aiden mocked. "The way Severn told it, you too were getting a bit too comfortable the other night. Severn was pretty pissed off when you ditched him to run off with Blondie. So you're not two-timing him with that one while we're in France?"

"Don't be so bloody ridiculous!" I was furious. "I never met the guy till we started on this show and I hadn't even spoken to him until we all went to McDonalds the other night. And if you remember correctly, it was because you lot wanted to get your own disgusting brand of take-aways that I went with the lighting guys in the first place. I had to get home somehow and I was hardly going to tag along and watch you lot play your revolting games with some poor unsuspecting drunk, was I? So don't get any more stupid ideas in your head and don't give me any more bullshit about 'my' boy racer."

"Are you and Severn okay?" Aiden asked quietly. "I kind of gathered something went wrong the other night between you.

Severn was in a very odd mood when he joined us."

"Joined you?" I spat. "Out hunting I presume?"

"Ye-es," Aiden nodded in reluctant admission.

"That's exactly what went wrong, if you really need to know, which you don't because it's actually none of your business. Like I told him, I can handle what you are, I just can't handle what it makes you do. It's gross! And vile! And disgusting! Now leave me alone and let me get finished."

I walked off leaving him staring at me like I had grown a second head.

By the time I had collected and coiled a whole lot more cables I had calmed down. I even managed a weak smile at Aiden although he pretended he hadn't noticed and scurried away in the opposite direction. My comments must have got to him. Good. His stupid comments about Cameron had got to me too. What I had said was true. I hadn't two-timed Severn with Cameron, but I had to admit that I had talked about him with Anita and I had thought about him quite a lot, even when I was with Severn, when I shouldn't have been thinking about him at all. Did thinking about him count in some way? Was it almost as bad as actually two-timing with him? I thought about how badly I had reacted to Severn's moves in the motel and I wondered what my reaction would have been if it had been Cameron. Would I have pushed him away? Was it only the blood-sucking part that turned me off or was I not as in love with Severn as I had thought I was? I was so busy with my thoughts I didn't notice Aiden slide up beside me.

"Juicy," he said in a surprisingly chilly tone.

"What?"

"That friend of the boy racer. Smells juicy. It's getting dark. Nearly supper time." He slurred the last two words into the way the evil Audrey plant sings it in the musical Little Shop of Horrors, which made it sound nasty, then he added a menacing chuckling laugh and slid away again into the darkness.

I tried not to let it get to me but it did, so when I got my final cables tidied away and saw Mum waiting for me by the car I breathed a sigh of relief.

"You finished?" she asked.

"Yeah, just stowed away the last of my stuff."

"Good. The opening night party is at the Mad Hatters' clubrooms. Grant and I are going, especially as Grant seems to be the official voice of the production now that Angus isn't here, so he will have to do the official speeches."

"Yay. Exciting."

"No, boring, but them's the joys of being the president's wife," Mum said in a fake American hillbilly accent. "Are you coming with me or waiting for the Men in Black? Oh, are they coming or are you all going off to execute the great retrieval plan?"

"There is no great retrieval plan" I admitted.

"But…"

"The Rev made it up. He just said that so Mr McCormack wouldn't do anything silly. He has no more idea of what to do next than we do."

"Oh." Mum sounded deflated, then paused to think before continuing. "In that case, let's get these opening night formalities out of the way as quickly as possible, then we can all sit down and work it out together. If Angus was promised action by tomorrow, there had better be some action. Round up the troops!"

Rounding up the vampires was the last thing I wanted to do. It had been a very long day, with all the running around searching for Tommy, followed by nearly five hours of rigging, operating then de-rigging a show I was getting sick of hearing. It might have been opening night but right at that moment I wished it was over. I didn't want to go to a party. I didn't want to pretend to be happy, which I wasn't. Most of all, after Aiden's creepy comments, I didn't want to see or talk to any vampires. I certainly didn't want to kiss one. I wanted to go home, but that wasn't going to happen. Mum already had me by the arm and was dragging me towards the container where the vampire trio and the lighting guys were loading the very last of the equipment. Aiden looked up, spotted me, looked over at Cameron who was talking to his unhelpful friend, turned back to me, gave an evil grin and licked his lips. I thought I was going to be sick. Mum must have noticed the stricken look on my face as she stopped walking and looked closely into my face.

"Are you okay?" she asked. "You don't look well."

Not for the first time recently I told her a lie.

"Just exhausted."

"Yes, I'm not surprised. It's been a long day. Let's round everyone up and get out of here."

CHAPTER TWENTY FOUR

The flat feeling must have been catching. The opening night party was more like a funeral. Instead of people laughing and congratulating each other, cast, crew and hangers-on stood in small groups, voices low, all talking about Tommy. Mum called it the 'elephant in the room'. We had only been there a few minutes before Grant dragged Mum away to circulate politely around the groups of people, which left me to do my usual party thing – I grabbed a couple of sandwiches and found a seat in a quiet corner where I could watch but stay out of the way.

The vampires were late and I could tell by the way they sent non-verbal messages to each other that something had happened. Severn's head started flicking from side to side as soon as he got through the door, so I guessed he was looking for me. I know I should have leaped up and gone to meet him but I just couldn't be bothered moving. Even for Severn. As his head swung back my way I put up my hand and waved, then felt guilty when I saw the huge smile break out on his face. I really should have rushed over to him instead of waiting like the Queen of England for him to come to me. Or maybe not. That would be so pathetic. Why shouldn't he rush to me? Oh, he did – from France. Or should we have rushed to each other like a slow-motion movie, with soaring music in the background? I settled for standing up and reaching out for the hug that I was soon enveloped in. That was good enough.

Still holding me tightly, Severn guided us to a convenient two-seater couch that a couple of older ladies had vacated and we snuggled up together, both wrapped in the folds of his huge black coat. I was quite happy just to stay there, not talking, but I could tell something had happened and I needed to know what it was. Even though I knew that as soon as I heard it I would wish that I didn't know, I still needed to know. How stupid was that? Finally I had to ask.

"What was going on with you guys when you arrived?"

"Nothing, why?" Severn looked genuinely confused.

"I don't know. I watched you guys walk in and I just had a funny feeling that something was up. The Rev and Aiden were giving each other funny looks, then looking at you and then back to each other. It just looked suspicious. Especially after Aiden and his weird, nasty comments at the show."

"What weird, nasty comments?" Severn's tone chilled.

I briefly considered not telling the truth, then thought "Stuff Aiden!"

"He was spouting off a whole load of bullshit about you thinking I was having it off with Cameron, which you had better not have been doing as it isn't true! Then we got onto you lot and your, um, meal preferences and I told Aiden what I've already told you, that it grosses me out. After that he got weird and started talking about how people looked 'juicy' and licking his lips. I know he was just doing it to wind me up, but he succeeded. I got wound up and I'm still wound up. He was quite creepy."

I should have shut up. But no, I have to open my mouth and tell it all, then wonder why the rollercoaster has started up again. Just when I am convincing myself that Severn is just a plain, ordinary, sexy, normal boyfriend, I tell him how I'm feeling and back comes the nasty side of the vampires. I could tell he was really angry. I could feel all his muscles tense up as his voice went menacingly quiet.

"Aiden!" He whispered it but I knew it would be heard where he intended. "When I get my hands on you, I'll…"

"Stop!" I put my hand on his chest. "Ignore it. He was just trying to wind me up. Let it go!"

Severn shut his eyes and I felt him slowly relax, consciously letting the anger drain away. I looked around, wondering where the other two were – I hadn't noticed them since they all arrived.

"They're over there," Severn must have been reading my mind, "behind the pot plant."

I looked harder and spotted them, barely noticeable in their black clothes, lurking in a dark corner well away from the milling crowd of actors. They must have heard Severn as they both looked at us at the same time. Aiden flicked his hand in a tiny wave so I gathered he had heard Severn's unfinished threat as well. He may even have replied but Severn wasn't letting on and I couldn't read anything in the grim look on his face.

Then Cameron arrived. I saw Aiden give a tiny smirk as he walked in. If he hadn't made that "juicy" comment earlier I wouldn't have noticed but the two things together made my hair stand on end. With a feeling of dread I realised that Cameron was by himself, not accompanied by the friend who had been sticking to him like glue all through the show. And why was he so late?

There was definitely something odd going on.

"Let's try this again," I said to Severn. "What is going on with you guys?"

"I have no idea," Severn replied. "Honestly, I have no idea what you're talking about. There is nothing 'going on', as you put it. Why are you so determined that there is?"

"Call it intuition. Maybe I am a bit like Mum. I can't explain it but something just feels wrong. Why was Cameron so late getting here? And where's the guy who was with him all evening?"

"I don't know," Severn said, "but there is one way to find out. Let's go and ask him." He pulled me up off the couch. "Cameron," he called out as he marched determinedly across the hall, me following in his wake. "Where have you been, mate?"

Cameron turned, looking a bit surprised at the enthusiastic welcome.

"Taking Braden home," he replied. "He wasn't well."

Severn shot me a smug look as if to say "I told you it was nothing" but something niggled at me.

"What happened?" I asked. "He looked fine when we were packing up."

"Yeah, he just passed out. Too much booze, I reckon. I'd left him waiting by my car while I went to get the last of the lighting rig. There was just me and," he pointed to Severn, "you guys left. Anyway, by the time I got the last load back to the container, Braden wasn't there. I thought he must have gone into the bushes for a pee so I called out but he didn't answer. I hunted through the bushes looking for him and I ran into the other two of you lot, sorry I can't remember their names, but they said they hadn't seen him. You guys left and I wandered around for a while wondering where the hell he had gone. So I rang his phone and heard it ringing, followed it and found him by the portaloos, lying on the ground. I nearly had a complete fit. I thought he was dead. But he wasn't and he came round just before I was about to ring for an ambulance. He must have put away a few more beers than we realised, because he couldn't remember even getting to the portaloos, let alone passing out."

"Is he all right now?" I asked, genuinely concerned but deeply suspicious of what I was hearing.

"Yeah, yeah, he'll be okay in the morning. He'll have a wicked headache and he's got a couple of scratches on his neck, but he'll live."

"Scratches on his neck?" I thought to myself, shooting a glare at Severn who picked up my thought, his forehead wrinkling into a worried frown.

"I'm glad he's going to be okay," I said hurriedly, tugging at Severn's arm as I spoke. "Come on, you, we have to find Mum. See ya later, Cameron."

Hoping I hadn't seemed rude to Cameron I dragged Severn away then pulled his face down to mine so I could whisper to him.

"Aiden bit him, didn't he?"

Severn let out a deep sigh. "It's possible. I didn't see it, but it's possible. Let's find them and ask."

We looked around the room to where the other two had previously been and, sure enough, they were still there, lounging against the wall, drinking from cans of coke. Aiden waved his can in the air. He was enjoying this.

"Yes I did," he exclaimed proudly as we approached. "Yum, yum, juicy!"

That did it! I stormed forward and shoved him in the chest.

"You piece of shit!" I spat. "How dare you!"

In a move much faster than I could react to, Aiden had grabbed my wrist, pulling me closer to him and holding me so tight I couldn't pull back without hurting myself. He was about to say something when he was stopped by Severn's arms reaching over the top of me and grabbing Aiden's wrists in a grip even tighter than the one he held me in.

"Let her go! Now!" he whispered, his voice soft but full of menace.

Aiden hesitated but gave in when Severn applied more pressure. I pulled my arm free, stepped behind Severn out of harm's way and waited to see who would throw the first punch and turn the whole thing into a public brawl. The two vampires stood eye to eye, glaring at each other and breathing heavily but before either could make a move the Rev stepped between them, a hand on each chest, pushing them apart.

"Calm down, both of you," he said quietly. "Aiden, as I told you before that was a really stupid thing to do. Stupid on several levels. And getting on Riley's bad side is even more stupid. There are not a lot of people we can trust and she's one we can. Considering how much she knows about us, you'd be pretty dumb to get her pissed off. So, apologise, nicely, and mean it!"

Aiden glared at him for a moment then threw his hands in

the air in a gesture of surrender.

"Okay. Sorry, Riley. I was stupid." He looked contritely down at his feet. "He just smelled so tasty. Sorry."

"Smelled tasty!" I shook my head in disbelief. "Bloody hell!" I looked at them all. "Whatever! Look, we still have to sort out what we are supposed to be doing about Tommy. Grant's going to be giving the official speeches soon then Mum wants us all to go home and figure out a plan, seeing you don't actually have one," I aimed the last comment at the Rev who nodded an admission of guilt. "But, quite frankly, right at this moment I don't actually want to talk to or be around any of you." I cut Severn off before he could start to argue. "Even you. You're all as bad as each other. You all do it. I need some space."

"Good idea," I heard the Rev say as I walked away. "Maybe we all need some space."

"Yeah, France might be far enough."

Funny, I hadn't thought Aiden's apology was very sincere. Leaving the vampires muttering to each other in the corner, I wandered outside for some fresh air and ran into Cameron, leaning against the wall, sneaking a cigarette.

"I really am sorry to hear about your friend," I opened the conversation. "I hope he will be okay."

"Yeah, he's an idiot. Serves him right. Weird marks though, looked like he'd been bitten by a vampire."

"Oh ha ha, like they would hang around Mona Vale. If they did you could get them to help you rig the lights."

"Lights and vampires? Nah! You could have them running sound out there in the dark. Come to think of it, your mates would make good vampires in those coats they wear."

"Ha ha again. Don't tell me you wouldn't kill for one of those coats when you're stuck up there on the followspot scaffold on a cold night."

"Yeah, true. They are pretty cool. I wonder if they could get me one. What do you reckon the story is with the kid? Have your parents found out who the mystery woman is yet?"

"Yeah." It wouldn't hurt to tell him some of the story. "Her name's Sally and one of the props ladies knew vaguely where she lived. We tracked that down but she's moved."

"Do you know where to?"

"Maybe." It was time to be very careful how much I said. "We think she's up in Westmoreland."

"Have you told the police that?"

"No," now I'm thinking fast. "We're not a hundred percent sure and we don't want to send the police on a wrong mission or have them barge in on some poor family that's got nothing to do with it."

"Fair enough. Hey, I don't know about you but I'm bored with this party – do you want to come for a drive? We could show me where you think she is and we could cruise past and take a look."

Oh, just like I did with the vampires earlier. "Okay."

"Not okay." Three black figures materialised out of the dark.

"Oh isn't it?" I glared at Severn, hands on my hips. "And you're going to stop me how?"

"Yeah, Cameron tried to sound tough. "You don't own her, mate! If she wants to ride with me, what's it to do with you?"

"Everybody calm down." The Rev stepped forwards. "We do not need the drama! There is no drama, so chill out you two. Riley, we would prefer that you don't drive away as we need you. Well, actually, your Mum needs you and we said we would find you. The official stuff is starting in there and your Mum needs your help."

"Oh, okay."

"See," the Rev looked pointedly between my two contesting males. "Now, if you two can stop strutting at each other like fighting roosters, we might be able to wrap this poor excuse for a party up and get away from here."

CHAPTER TWENTY FIVE

The Rev wasn't the only one happy to leave the party early. Almost as soon as Grant had finished his thank-you speeches, people started to say their goodbyes and leave. Usually opening night parties were noisy affairs with lots of singing and dancing, and the occasional illegal use of pyrotechnics, that went on until almost sunrise, but this party would itself up in record time. There was even food left uneaten. Waste not, want not, as my Grandmother used to say – I grabbed a couple of serviettes, wrapped up a variety of sandwiches, biscuits and savouries and tried to look innocent as I carried them out the door. As I climbed into the car, Mum gave me a strange look and I thought she was going to tell me off until she unwrapped her own collection of left-overs and I realised that she had done the same. At least we would have food to fuel our brains while we came up with the master plan to rescue Tommy.

Back at our place, the vampires draped their coats over the back of the kitchen chairs while Mum, Grant and I threw our stolen food onto plates and made coffee. Once we were all sitting down, Grant opened the conversation.

"Right! We had better come up with a plan fast because if Tommy doesn't get safely home soon we may as well wrap this show up and close it down, if tonight is anything to go by."

"It wasn't that bad," Mum argued.

"No, it was worse! It was probably the worst opening night I have ever been part of. Nobody was concentrating on giving a good performance, except us of course. All anyone could talk about was Tommy. Quite frankly I am sick to death of this kid – he sabotaged the show with his bad acting and appalling manners when he was there and now he's not there, instead of having a better show, we've got a worse one! I spent the first few weeks of this show wanting him gone, now I just want him back as soon as possible so we can all get on with some acting."

"Tell us how you really feel." Severn laughed.

"Oh come on! You must agree with me. Tonight was a disaster."

"I'm not disagreeing," Severn replied. "It was pretty bad. So what are we going to do? Rev?"

"Well," the Rev suggested. "We could start by going up

there again tonight. If I remember rightly, all those houses up the top back onto paddocks with horses in them, so we should be able to sneak down the back without anyone seeing us. You never know there might be a way in."

"So we sneak in like a team of second–rate commandos, and then what?" Aiden sounded unconvinced. Or maybe he was still pissed with being told off by the Rev earlier.

"It depends," the Rev answered. "We might get lucky. She might be out and we might be able to grab Tommy and go."

"Or not."

"Or not," the Rev agreed. "But we won't know until we try."

"It's two-storey," Severn remembered. "When I went to the front door I was pretty sure I could hear Tommy upstairs. Have you still got the photo of the street view?"

Grant reached around to find the photo in a pile of papers on the sideboard behind him and placed it on the table. Severn studied the picture and continued.

"I'm pretty sure he's in a room around the back. The noise definitely wasn't from one of those front rooms."

"That makes sense," the Rev agreed. "She wouldn't want anyone seeing him through a window and out the back there're only the horses."

"And they can't call the police," Severn finished for him. "So, what do you want to do?"

The Rev looked at his watch.

"It's nearly midnight. I think we should head up there and have a look around."

Mum held up a hand in a stop gesture. "Before you rush off, let's just recap what we know for sure and what we are guessing. We know the strange woman who was hanging around the show hasn't been there since Tommy disappeared. We know that up until a couple of days ago she lived in Beckenham, just around the corner from the McCormacks. We know she is now in Ravensdale Rise. But we are only guessing that she is, in fact, the same woman who gave birth to Tommy. We are only guessing that she has him stashed away up there. We may be completely wrong. We may be right, but we may be wrong. So please remember that before you all do something stupid, and illegal, like breaking into her house." She glared pointedly at the three vampires and, again, we all knew that she knew their secret. "I'm sure you don't want to get yourselves arrested," she finished.

"No way!" Severn nodded in agreement. "No way!"

"We're not going to break in, we're going to reconnoitre," the Rev assured Mum.

"But if there was a window conveniently open…" Aiden gave her a sweet, innocent smile that didn't fool any of us. Mum closed her eyes and cradled her head in her hands.

"I don't want to know. Just be careful and remember that she lives there legally, you don't. If she catches you and rings the police, even if she has kidnapped Tommy, you guys are still going to be arrested. Don't. Do. Anything. Stupid!"

"So what are we going to do?" I asked.

"Like I said before, we're going to head up there and suss the place out," the Rev replied, determining the action by standing up and grabbing his coat. "Come on, you three, let's go."

"Riley doesn't need to go, does she?" Mum asked, horrified at the thought.

"Yes, she does. If Tommy is there, he knows Riley. She's dealt with his radio mic for weeks. He'll trust her. He's only met me once and he doesn't know Severn or Aiden at all. If we need to get him out quietly, Riley's going to be essential." He looked closely at the concerned expression on Mum's face. "Don't worry. We'll look after her."

Leaving her no chance to argue, I grabbed my jacket and hurried out the door. Actually I was excited. If the vampires were going on a mission that didn't include sucking someone's blood, there was no way I was being left out.

CHAPTER TWENTY SIX

We parked the rental car at the very top of the hill, on the curve where the road stopped, facing back down the hill for a fast getaway, then slipped quietly over the fence into the paddock. Fortunately the moon wasn't full and we were past the streetlights so in our black backstage clothes we were almost invisible. The vampires moved so quietly. I felt that I was the only one making any noise as we crept down the paddock. How long would it be before I could move with such stealth? It could be a useful skill to have. As my nylon jacket rustled as I moved, I realised how good those long coats of theirs actually were. Ideal cover in the darkness, completely silent, warm and loaded with chocolate. I must get one.

We slipped past the backs of the houses, watching for lights in windows or, a worse threat, guard dogs that would bark a warning. As we passed the third house I nearly had a heart attack as a cat raced across the grass in front of me, leaping up onto the boundary fence and into the house's back garden. The Rev heard my gasp of surprise, smothered a laugh and gave me a reassuring pat on my shoulder. I breathed deeply and carried on, carefully watching where I put my feet, avoiding potholes and horse manure.

Then we were outside our target. Unlike the house where the cat went, this one had no fancy fence, just a simple one made of wire mesh, so it was an easy task to clamber over it into the back yard. There was a light on in a corner window which, judging by its box shape, was probably where the kitchen was. The Rev put a finger to his mouth to indicate that we should be quiet then whispered something in a voice so low I couldn't hear him. Aiden and Severn obviously did as they both nodded then Aiden slipped away across the lawn towards the light. I shivered, more from the adrenalin rush than from cold. Severn noticed, put his arm around me and smiled. As he looked down at me I could see, even in the dark, that his eyes were abnormally bright, flicking hurriedly from side to side, taking in everything. The vampires were in hunting mode. I shivered again.

"Come on, Aiden wants us," the Rev whispered in my ear.

We made our way carefully across the lawn to join Aiden who was crouched under the lit-up window.

"Listen," he whispered.

Even my human ears could hear the woman crying. Severn's ears picked up another sound. He tapped the Rev on the shoulder and gestured upwards. Someone else was upstairs, but was it Tommy? Severn look around, smiling as he took in the design of the house which offered a flat-roofed garage with a convenient deck on the roof leading to what was probably the master bedroom. He handed me his coat then deftly climbed the garage wall like a cat. I wondered how as there were no hand or foot holds that I could see – he seemed to shimmy up the flat side like Spiderman. Then, in a lightening-quick move that made him seem nothing more than a passing shadow, he was at the other side of the deck, crouching behind a deck chair. Another blur of movement and he was at the very edge, as close as he could get to the room he was interested in. I could just make him out in the darkness, pressing his head against the house wall, presumably listening.

At the Rev's whispered command the three of us on the ground moved back across the lawn to regroup by the fence, joined minutes late by Severn who pulled on his coat and confirmed that Tommy was asleep in the upstairs bedroom.

"How do you know it's him?" I asked, making Severn smile.

"He's snoring. Same tonal vibrations." I must have looked disbelieving. "If you can trust Aiden on the smell thing, you can trust me on sound. I'll stake my career as a sound technician on it being him."

"Stake is not a good term for a vampire to use," I grinned, "but I'll believe you. So what's next? Want do we do now?"

"I have an idea," the Rev said, his voice still a tiny whisper. "If she's crying, maybe she's regretting her actions and maybe I can play on that. Let's see if I can get us through the door. Aiden, come with me. Severn, your job is to watch the back until we're inside in case she bolts for it, then Aiden will let you in and you and Riley can get upstairs and grab the boy – without making him scream, we don't want to alert the neighbours. If I can talk her around, we can take him out without any problem. If I can't, you'll have to grab him and run and leave her to Aiden and me. Okay? Follow me!"

I shook my head. "You reckon? You honestly think she's going to let you lot in? Come on!"

"Do you have a better idea?"

"Maybe. She might open the door to me. If I tell her I have

a message from the McCormacks, and she thinks it's just me, she might let me in – it's worth a try."

"I agree. Let's try it."

That was our first mistake.

Our second mistake was deciding that the vampires should wait hidden in the back yard until I was in and could open a door or a window to let them in too. But I didn't know those were mistakes until it was too late. Until then, I thought I had the easy job. I just had to talk her into opening the door. I sneaked around the side of the house then straightened up and walked normally to the front door and knocked.

There was no answer. I waited about thirty seconds then knocked again, louder. Sure enough, the door cracked open and a face appeared in the gap. I broke into my hastily prepared speech.

"Sally? I'm Riley Lowe, I've seen you at Mona Vale. The McCormacks have asked me to bring you a message. I know all about Tommy and I know why you have him. I would like to come in and talk about it with you. I'm on your side and I want to help."

I guess what happened next just proves you shouldn't tell lies, because the "I'm on your side" lie bit me on the bum very quickly. Without speaking, Sally reached out, grabbed my arm and pulled me inside, locking the door behind me. If the vampires had planned to follow me in, they weren't coming in through the front door.

I smiled. Non-threatening. She glared, squeezed my arm tighter and pushed me down the passage into the kitchen which turned out to be a fabulously glamorous affair with granite benches and gleaming stainless steel appliances. Mum would kill for a kitchen like that. It didn't go at all with Sally's style so I figured she must be renting, furniture and all. She pushed me towards a black wrought-iron chair at the end of a mammoth black-topped dining table.

"You!" she gasped. "You're from that show. I've seen you. You," she poked me in the chest, "you're the girl who was mean to Joshua."

"Joshua?" I was confused. Did we have it that wrong?

"Yes, that's his name. He's not Tommy. His name's Joshua. They promised they would call him that, then they changed it. I hate Tommy. He's not a Tommy. He's Joshua."

"Okay, okay, he's Joshua, I can live with that."

."What do you want? You said you had a message from

them." She spat the word "them" out like it was poisoned. "Get on with it then. What have they got to say? How much money are they offering this time?"

"Um," it was time to think fast. "Um, can I please have a glass of water? It was a long walk up the hill."

"You walked? You haven't got a car?"

"No, do I look old enough to have my own car?" I biked, but my bike is down the hill, I got sick of pushing it up the steep bits."

She fell for that lie – but, again, tell lies, something worse happens. It wasn't a glass she took out of a cupboard, it was a long, rather evil-looking knife. All I could think to say as she stuck it into the side of my neck was, "oh shit."

At least she didn't stick it in far. I could feel the point and I knew she had drawn blood but I didn't think I was going to bleed to death. But it hurt! She was obviously crazy and my only help was outside.

Downside – I was locked in a house with a crazy lady with a knife.

Upside – there were three vampires outside who could hear me.

Solution – keep talking and play for time, so while the crazy lady tied my hands behind my back with a large cable tie, dragged me upstairs by my ponytail and pushed me into a wardrobe in a bedroom, I kept up a running commentary on the action.

"Why are you doing this? Why are you tying my hands behind my back? Why are we going upstairs? What room is this? Why are you locking me in a wardrobe?"

Okay, I shouted the last bit, but more to make her reply than to let the vampires here me. Then I wished I hadn't asked.

"To get rid of you," she answered. "By the time anyone figures you're missing, Joshua and I will be long gone and by the time they find you, you will have starved to death. You'll be a bag of bones on the floor."

Sweet!

"Bullshit! My parents know exactly where I am. So do the McCormacks. I phoned them just before I knocked. If I don't phone them back in fifteen minutes, they'll call the police."

That was all bullshit but I wished it was true.

"Doesn't take fifteen minutes to bleed to death!" Sally waved the knife for emphasis but before she could stick it into me, I was saved by the bell. Well, a knock on the front door actually.

Growling like a dog, Sally stuffed the knife into the pocket of the scruffy dressing gown she was wearing over old pyjamas, slammed the wardrobe door and plunged me into darkness.

If I had clocked up a few stupidity points already, this time the points went to Sally. You can't lock someone in a wardrobe with a sliding door! Even with my hands tied behind me it was easy enough to push it open with my feet and my head, so I wasn't far behind her by the time she opened the door. I watched and listened from the top of the stairs. Of course it was vampires at her door – who else calls at midnight? I heard the Rev speak.

"Sally? I'm the Reverend David Rochester. I'm a minister of the church and I'm here to help you. I know all about Tommy and I know all about the problems you have. I would like to come in and talk about it with you. I know I can help."

The Rev could sell snow to penguins, and then sell them a fridge to keep it in. The strangely hypnotic tone to his soft voice must have been the real thing because it seemed to do the trick. She let him in. I couldn't believe it. I mean, a tiny little guy not much taller than a kid, looking like a reject from a science fiction movie, knocks on your door in the middle of the night and just because he says he's a minister, with nothing to prove it, the silly woman lets him in? What was she thinking? He could've been a serial killer. Or a vampire. I watched in amazement as she opened the door wider, then followed as he turned to beckon us to follow him inside.

Sally gasped in terror as Aiden and Severn appeared from the darkness and crammed into the tiny hallway. Her eyes flicked from person to person, taking in their blackness, then she gasped again as recognition set in.

The Rev put a hand gently against her back and began to guide her through to the kitchen.

"Come on, let's all sit down and talk about this."

"You're not a minister," she repeated as they entered the kitchen. "Why did you say you were?"

"Because I am," the Rev replied, maintaining the gently hypnotic voice he used at the door. "I am the Reverend Father David Rochester from the Mountain of Angels Monastery."

"But you were working at that show. I saw you."

"Yes, I am. Because… because," he stumbled for a plausible reason, "because our monastery requires us to do community work as part of our outreach." He hurried on before she thought too much about his answer. "But, enough about us, I can see that you've been crying, your eyes are all red. I think that you have done something that you regret, am I right? Because if that's the case, we are here to make it right. Would you like to tell us why you took Tommy?"

CHAPTER TWENTY SEVEN

Much as I wanted to hear what the Rev was doing, I had more important things to do, like getting my hands untied and finding Tommy. Fortunately, Severn had the same idea and had raced straight up the stairs. Like all good backstage crew he had a craft knife in his pocket, so the cable tie was gone in an instant, freeing my hands to give my rescuer a hug, then a kiss. We both thought about another kiss but both us pulled away to concentrate on the job we were supposed to be concentrating on. Finding Tommy. Severn led the way down the hall to a back room. The door was locked but as it was to keep Tommy in, not keep Sally out, the key was conveniently in the lock.

"New lock," Severn commented. "Not the usual sort to have on the outside of a bedroom door."

He turned the key and we crept slowly inside, not wanting to have Tommy wake up in fright. We needn't have bothered. He was sound asleep. Severn pointed to a small bottle on the bedside cabinet.

"Drugged," he said quietly. "Damn. We need to wake him up,"

"I'll try." I sat on the bed beside Tommy and shook his shoulder. "Stand by beginners, Act one. Beginners on stage now."

Tommy mumbled something incomprehensible and squirmed in the bed. I tried again in a firmer voice.

"Tommy! You're needed on stage. Stop slacking around and get your microphone on right now! The stage manager's waiting for you and she's very angry."

There is nothing like the fear of the stage manager's wrath to get actors to move. Tommy wriggled and his eyes fluttered. I shook him again.

"Come on, Tommy, wake up!"

I continued to work frantically on Tommy, desperately trying to get him to respond as the noises from downstairs got louder. By the sound of it we were running out of time. Severn slipped back downstairs to see how the Rev was doing with our kidnapper, but came back a few minutes later, not looking too happy.

"I think we need to get him out of here as fast as possible," he said. "She's nuts. One sentence she's all calm, agreeing with the Rev that she's made a terrible mistake and that 'Joshua' won't do what she tells him and keeps hitting her and she doesn't know what to do; next sentence she's raving how she'll kill them both before she lets anyone take him away again."

"Shit! Come on, Tommy, you have to wake up, you have to go home!"

"Home," Tommy finally responded. He looked up at me, real fear in his eyes. "I want to go home," he whimpered.

"Home," I repeated. "We've come to get you. We're taking you home. You just need to wake up."

Tommy struggled to sit up in the bed. "I want to see my Mum," he cried. "I don't want to be here with her. She's mad. She thinks I'm someone else. She calls me Joshua and … and ... and she makes me eat broccoli. I want my Mum."

Severn was only half listening as he was more tuned into what he was hearing from downstairs.

"Don't worry about her," he reassured Tommy. "We won't let her near you. But it seems we have a slight problem."

Again, I didn't need vampire ears to work out what was happening. Crazy Sally must have worked herself into a state and was now, from the sound of it, standing at the foot of the stairs, shouting defiance and refusing to let Tommy be brought down. I gathered from his menacing tones that Aiden was above her on the stairs stopping her coming up, but that didn't solve our problem of getting down and safely out the door.

I heard Sally's voice change from swearing and threatening to crying and pleading, then she wound up into the start of a piercing shriek, suddenly cut off by a smack and a forceful "shut up" from Aiden. Sally was crying again, softer than before. Then the Rev's voice again, reminding her that the police were looking for her and would arrest her for kidnapping and I gathered from the look on Severn's face that he didn't want to be anywhere near if the police arrived. Which they might soon if Sally didn't turn down her volume which was escalating rapidly back to screeching level. From the second smack I figured Aiden had hit her again. I shook my head at Severn.

"What are we going to do? She's going nuts and we can't let Aiden beat her up. How do we get past her?"

"Just like this." Severn moved to the side of the bed, scooping Tommy into his arms. "Hang on tight, kid."

It should have been easy. Walk down the stairs, let Aiden sort the crazy lady and get out the door. But no. I had to stuff it up.

If I had been thinking I would have let Severn go first – after all, I wasn't the one who needed to get out. But I was closest to the door so I went down the stairs ahead of Severn, passed Aiden and straight into Crazy Sally. Stupid, stupid, stupid!

One second I was walking down the stairs then a second later I was twisting sideways, a wiry but very strong hand hauling me by my ponytail. Again! Before the normally speedy vampires could react and before I could regain my balance, I felt a shark prick on the side of my neck. The knife. Again!

"Stop!" Crazy Sally's in charge now. She glared up at Severn, still holding Tommy at the top of the stairs. "Put Joshua back to bed or I will slit her throat! Do it now!"

"Okay," Severn backed off. I could see the Rev's eyes flickering from one of us to the other, calculating his next move. Aiden, on the other hand, gave me that horrid grin of his that said he was enjoying himself.

"Sally," the Rev turned his smooth hypnotic tone on full bore. "Joshua's fine. He's going back to bed. Now, we can see that you're upset, but hurting Riley won't help. Let's go back into the kitchen where we can all sit down and have a nice cup of tea and talk about it."

Cup of tea? I've got a knife sticking into my neck and you think a cup of tea is going to fix it? You don't even drink tea!

It worked though. Sort of. Sally caught onto the idea of getting off the stairs but not the going into the kitchen nicely bit. Her idea of nice was dragging me by my hair, knife drawing blood as it stuck in a bit deeper with every step, to the bottom of the stairs and into the passage by the front door where she hauled me around until we blocked the exit. The Rev and Aiden followed carefully and I could just see Severn's shoes still at the top of the stairs.

The blood was starting to run down my neck. Aiden licked his lips. Oh hell, they were already in hunting mode, what if the blood tipped them over the edge and the whole rescue-Tommy plan got turned into a lets-eat-Riley frenzy. I put my hand to my neck to wipe the blood away with my fingers. Dumb move! Crazy Sally growled and pressed the knife harder.

"Okay, okay," I spluttered. "Chill out!" I looked at the vampires, trying to buy some time before she whipped the knife across my throat and I bled out on the floor. Now I was wishing I had become a vampire already – I would have had a few more options for getting free than the absolutely none that I had. "Hey look, Sally, T..Joshua's okay. He's back in bed. He's all yours. You can keep him. Let me go and we can just leave. We can all pretend we've never been here and you can take him away to the Coromandel or wherever you want to go."

"No!" She wasn't buying it. "If you go now, you'll send the police. I can't have that." The knife stuck in again.

"No we won't," the Rev cut in. "We all know that if the police come, the boy will be taken away from all of you – the child welfare people will take him away and none of you will ever see him again. We know the adoption was illegal. Like I said before, let's see if we can help you." The Rev's voice dropped again into smooth hypnotist mode. "We're on your side here. We want to help."

But Crazy Sally wasn't that crazy. She didn't believe him either. I knew she didn't because the knife moved from the side of my neck to the front – one false move now and I was history. Up at the top of the stairs I saw Severn's shoes start to descend.

"No! Stop! If she feels threatened she's going to kill me!" I didn't shout that, even though I wanted to. I whispered it, really quietly, which is as good as a shout to the vampires. Severn stopped. He was now far enough down the stairs that I could see his face. I'm sure he winked.

"Sally," he called softly. "Can you come and see Joshua please – he's asking for you."

Sally hesitated. The knife's pressure eased off. Severn asked again.

"Please. He needs you."

Sally bought it. With the knife firmly attached to my throat and my head tilted sideways as she still gripped my ponytail, I was pushed ahead of her up the stairs. A re-run of the first time. The Rev stepped back towards the kitchen, letting her go. Aiden stayed where he was on the stairs but flattened himself against the wall so we could pass. Then he moved. In the fraction of a second when Sally looked down at her feet, Aiden was between us, grabbing her knife hand, pushing it into the air and shoving me forwards to safety. Then another hand reached out to grab me and I was at the top of the stairs in Severn's arms. He tilted my head gently to the side and licked the blood from my neck. I let him.

Down the stairs the Rev had taken over. Aiden had pushed

Sally against the wall. He tossed the knife down the stairs where the Rev had picked it up and stuffed it into a coat pocket.

"What shall we do now?" he asked.

Sally's answer was to come back fighting. She aimed a swift accurate kick at Aiden's shin. He swore. I might have got away from the knife but she wasn't giving up easily. I couldn't see how we were going to get Tommy down the stairs and out the door.

Severn's head flicked from side to side – I could almost see his brain ticking over, thinking through the positions of the windows and doors, figuring out an exit strategy.

"I'll get Tommy out of here," Severn said both to me and to the vampires downstairs. "I'll leave you to deal with her, but I'm flying him out."

"You're what?" I only heard myself ask that but I think Severn heard it from three mouths.

"I'm flying him out. It'll work. It's pitch black out there, no-ones going to see me and if they do, they'll think I'm some kind of crazy hang-glider pilot. The kid's half doped with some kind of sedative. He's not going to remember much of this and even if he tells everyone that a man with wings flew him down the hill to safety, who's going to believe him? They'll put it down to hallucinations from the drugs. Anyway, that's what I'm doing. Right now! Riley, you get to look after my clothes. I'll meet you in that park at the bottom of the hill and don't take too long – I want my clothes back soonest."

The sound of Sally swearing at Aiden and trying to push past him up the stairs sealed the deal. As Severn stripped off his coat and t-shirt, I got Tommy off the bed, laughing in spite of the panic when I saw that he was dressed in childish pyjamas with fire engines on them, and slid his feet into a pair of cute doggy slippers I found on the floor. Her taste in boys' clothes was as bad as her taste in skirts. The drugs she had him sedated with were still working well and it was almost impossible to keep him sitting up, let alone helping himself, but I managed. Once I had his slippers on, Severn scooped him up in his arms, I grabbed Severn's coat and t-shirt, and we hurried down the passage to the master bedroom.

"Hang on tight," Severn told Tommy as he stepped through the sliding door onto the deck, stood firmly with his feet apart and flexed his shoulders. I watched in awe as his huge, creamy, leather wings unfurled from the centre of his back, spreading the full width of the deck. I had seen their wings before, in the theatre last year, but it was still an amazingly impressive and slightly scary sight. I could understand why the French farmers might think they were angels. Maybe they were. Maybe vampires and angels were the same thing. I could tell myself that – I wasn't becoming a vampire, I was becoming an angel. I heard Tommy gasp as, with a few beats to warm up, Severn stepped off the edge of the deck and soared upwards into the black depths of the Port Hills night.

CHAPTER TWENTY EIGHT

By the time Aiden had given in and let Sally up the stairs, I had locked the sliding door, closed the room and was back in Tommy's room trying to look innocent. Sally burst in then stopped in her tracks as she saw the empty bed.

"Where is he?" she demanded. "What have you done with Joshua?"

"Tommy," I said. "Not Joshua. He's gone home. Where he belongs. It's over."

"Nooooo!" Sally collapsed into a ball on the floor. "Noooo!"

Aiden stepped forwards to drag her unceremoniously to her feet, almost throwing her onto the bed.

"You stay here," he ordered. "I'll be back for you."

I grabbed Severn's clothes and we left the room, closing the door on Sally who had curled herself up on Tommy's bed.

"Are you really coming back?" I asked Aiden.

"Yes he is," the Rev replied for him. "I want him to get it through her head that her best option is to leave town. He's good at that sort of persuasion."

"Okay," I didn't want to think too deeply about how that persuasion was persuaded. "In that case, let's give ourselves a head start." I locked the bedroom door.

"Nice," Aiden applauded.

This time we left by the front door, walking as innocently as possible up the street to the car. Well, as innocent as three people in black clothes, two looking like Matrix extras, can possibly look. I breathed a sigh of relief once we were safely in the car and driving down the hill.

"Where's this park?" Aiden asked.

I gave him directions and we were there in record time. There was no sign of Severn.

"Are you sure this is where he meant us to meet him?" Aiden sounded anxious.

"Yes, I'm sure. He'll be here somewhere. He's probably hiding out – it's not like he's going to wander around in public with no shirt on and his wings out."

We sat and waited for what seemed like ages but was probably only a few minutes, before the Rev indicated that he heard him. I got out of the car just as there was a whoosh of rushing air and a large human-shaped albatross landed cleanly in the centre of the small park. By the time I had turned to get his T-shirt and coat from the car, Severn had furled his wings and was running towards us. A quick hug of relief and he was pulling on his t-shirt and reaching for the can of coke the Rev was holding out to him.

"Where's Tommy?" I asked the obvious question. "I thought you were bringing him here. You didn't drop him or anything?"

"No, I didn't drop him," Severn laughed. "He's quite safe. I landed him in the Beckenham school grounds which, as you know, is just a couple of blocks from his house."

"But he's drugged up to the eyeballs," I spluttered. "You can't leave him in a school!"

"Believe me, by the time we had flown down the hill, he was awake. I landed him in the school playground and we had a little talk. We came to an agreement. He knows what just happened but there is no way he is going to tell anyone because he knows that no-one will believe him and I told him that, if he does, Riley will find out and we will come after him and turn him into a vampire, or suck all his blood out till he's a corpsicle."

"And just how am I supposed to hear about it if he tells someone?"

"I don't know. I told him that you would know and he believed me. He thinks you're a vampire too and, even if he didn't think that, he is way more scared of you than he is of us. One threat of Riley with a roll of gaffer tape and he'll do anything."

I laughed. "So what's he doing now?"

"He's walking home. He should be there by now. More of our cover story – he's going to tell everyone that he escaped all by himself and ran home. He doesn't know exactly where he was on the hill, so he doesn't have to tell any lies; he's just going to say that he got out behind her back and ran as fast as he could to the bottom of the hill, then recognised where he was and walked home. The police are bound to ask him questions but I'm sure Heidi will stop them questioning him too much. What have you done with the crazy woman?"

"She's locked in the bedroom. Aiden's dropping us back to Riley's then he's going back up to let her out and convince her to get the hell out of town and never come back," the Rev explained.

"How's he going to do that?"

"Pay her off. It worked before. He can work out a deal, text me her bank details and I'll have the money in there straight away. If McCormack could work out a deal that shut her up for ten years, I can make an offer that will last a lifetime."

That was true. I had already figured out that the Rev must be a multi-millionaire. Seven hundred years worth of savings and the ownership of a large amount of French land must make him pretty comfortable.

"Let's go home," I broke in. "I bet Mum and Grant are still waiting up for us."

Which was also true. Mum greeted us at the door with a huge smile for everyone and a hug for me. Grant was on the phone, obviously to Mr McCormack, also grinning from ear to ear.

"I don't know what you did, but whatever it was, it was brilliant," Mum enthused. "Angus is on the phone. Tommy turned up on their doorstep ten minutes ago. Apparently he's wearing pyjamas and is very confused, but he's safe home. He's saying that he escaped but ... did he have some help?"

"We can neither confirm nor deny that he may, or may not, have had some assistance in fleeing the establishment," the Rev laughed. "Let's just say that we may, or may not, have some knowledge of what went on, but we will deny that if officially asked."

"Where's Aiden?" Mum asked.

"On a mission, tidying up a few loose ends," was the Rev's enigmatic reply.

Grant hung up the phone, smiling broadly.

"Come on, we know that wasn't a coincidence – you lot going up there and Tommy miraculously reappearing. Tell us what really happened."

The Rev relented and over the coffees thrust at us by Mum he told as much of the story as was possible, editing out the Severn flying off bit in favour of letting them think that Severn merely carried him to the car. He also edited the bit where Severn dropped him in the school grounds to walk himself home and let them think that we dropped him off on the corner of his street, within sight of his house. We understood why Severn had chosen the school as a good place to land, but Mum wouldn't understand him leaving Tommy there. We could hardly explain that Severn was, at the time, shirtless and could hardly walk the streets of Beckenham with his wings on display.

As the Rev's story neared its end, Mum looked at her watch.

"Right, that's enough for now," she ordered. "It is now

about the time I would have been expecting us to get home from the opening night party, which means it's sleep time. We have a long day tomorrow – a matinee and an evening show so, with all the good will in the world, guys, go away. Brunch here at 11am if you're awake and if you're hungry. Pancakes and maple syrup."

Severn and the Rev nodded their agreement and stood up to leave, promising to be back for pancakes in the morning.

"Damn, looks like we're walking," the Rev complained as I walked them outside.

"I wonder how Aiden's getting on?" I pondered the question we were all thinking.

"He'll be fine," the Rev assured. "He's good at this sort of thing. Whatever it takes to make sure she's not a problem that's likely to return, he'll do it."

As I hugged Severn goodbye I wasn't sure if I was reassured by that or worried.

CHAPTER TWENTY NINE

I wasn't any more reassured the next morning. Severn turned up by himself for Mum's pancake brunch, telling us that Aiden and the Rev were still asleep, but something in the way he said it made me not quite believe him. He had walked from the motel and I just had a funny feeling that Aiden and the Rev weren't hanging sleepily from the motel wardrobe rails like good little vampire bats, but were actually out somewhere in the car doing something I didn't want to think about. Still, I suppose I would have to get used to the fact that my boyfriend and his friends had a rather unique taste in breakfast that maple syrup wasn't going to fulfil. I didn't ask.

Mum and I hadn't managed to sleep in – the phone had been going crazy all morning as cast members rang to share the good news. It appeared that Tommy had stuck to the story he had arranged with Severn and there was no mention of strange flying men with wings. By the sound of it, he had even embellished the story with explicit, if imagined, details of running around streets, imagining Sally was chasing him, hiding in bushes when he heard people coming and all sorts of other details that made his escape a very dramatic story of bravery and heroism. His fifteen minutes of fame were now even better than he would have got from his role in Robin Hood and this time his acting was better as everyone was believing him.

I was more interested in finding out how Aiden had got on with Sally but no-one except Severn knew that Aiden had been on a mission to get rid of her and Severn wasn't telling – if he even knew. When I got a chance I pulled Severn into Grant's office for a quiet chat.

"Aiden and the Rev aren't really at the motel sleeping, are they?" I asked.

"Um, no. I have no idea where they are. Aiden arrived back at the motel about an hour after we got back, woke up the Rev and they went off again together."

"What did they say to each other? You must have heard something."

"No. They know I can hear better than they can. Aiden made bloody sure I wasn't in on whatever they're up to."

"Maybe they've just gone to transfer money to Sally and, I don't know, take her to the airport and get her on a plane."

"Yes, that's probably it. Anyway, we'll know soon enough. They'll be at Mona Vale by pack-in time. They won't miss that."

He was right. They were late but they arrived. Severn and I had already laid out half the cables and were starting to place the speakers when they finally showed up, apologising profusely but not offering any explanations. Not that there was any time to listen to them. It was a mad rush to get everything set up in time for our first matinee, which was obviously popular as audience started arriving not long after we did, complicating our job as we had to work around them.

Over in the dressing tents the atmosphere was electric. It had all the excitement and atmosphere that opening night was lacking. The talk was, once again, all about Tommy but this time it was cheerful, happy talk as the cast and crew swapped their bits of information on his miraculous return. Fortunately we were not mentioned.

On one of my trips back to the container for equipment, I ran into Cameron and dared to ask how his mate, Braden, was.

"Completely washed out," Cameron replied. "I went around to his place this morning and he looks like shit. Really pale. He says he feels faint and dizzy if he gets up too quickly. His mum's making him stay in bed today and if he's not better by tomorrow she's going to drag him off to the doctor."

"Oh, that's no good. I hope he'll be okay."

"Yeah, he will be. Between you and me, I reckon it wasn't just the booze. I reckon he must have taken something else as well."

"What? Like drugs?" At least if Cameron thought that, nobody would look for other reasons and start asking awkward questions about the marks on his neck.

"Yeah, he must have. Serves him right if it made him sick."

We collected the equipment we had gone to the container to collect and hurried in different directions to set it up, so I didn't see Cameron again until the show had begun. By that time we were both on our towers, me tucked in beside Severn, Cameron higher up, lashed by a safety chord to his followspot. There was nothing I could do for his friend but at least I knew he would recover from Aiden's nasty little attack. Juicy indeed! Which got me thinking – I wonder if he had snacked on Sally as well. I mean, why not? He would have been alone in her house, no-one to stop him. Maybe the Rev joined him. I could see them doing that and not telling Severn in case he told me. And if they had, did I care? Sally wasn't a very nice person. Oh, and that wasn't a very nice thought. She must have been a nice person once. I thought of Anita and how she might turn out if someone forced her to sell them her baby. In spite of the yelling and threats last night, Sally deserved sympathy, not abuse. I sincerely hoped the boys hadn't snacked on her, but I would take bets that they had.

Not that I had any time to dwell on it. From the minute the stage manager called 'beginners' there was no time to think about anything except the show, which ran in high gear. The energy from the actors was electrifying, firing up the musicians and the audience. If the opening night had been like a bad second show, the matinee had all the energy of an opening night. When I went backstage at interval the dressing rooms were jumping. I started looking forward to the evening show, even more so when it was announced that, to celebrate Tommy's return, there would be another party.

Fired up on a mixture of adrenalin, chocolate and cans of coke, we bounced through the second half, clapping along with the audience as the actors took two curtain calls. Then it was over, the audience packed up their deck chairs, rugs and picnic baskets and wandered away. All that was left for us to do was to work out who was volunteering to stay behind and guard the equipment during the three-hour break until the evening performance. Funnily enough, none of the vampires were keen to stay out in the sun any longer than they had to, so we were all glad when Danny volunteered to stay if someone would bring him beer and McDonalds, which Cameron offered to do, leaving us free to leave and head home for a well-earned rest.

CHAPTER THIRTY

I didn't go home. Mum and Grant just waved to me as they past through the carpark and left me with Severn, so that's where I went – back to the motel, via the pizza shop. It was lovely to have nothing to do for a couple of hours except enjoy being with my boyfriend, even if it was in a small space with two other vampires watching our every move. It was also the best opportunity I would get to ask the Rev some important but difficult questions. I started with the most recent.

"What happened to Sally? Did you pay her off? Has she gone?"

'Yes, she's gone," Aiden replied. "She will not be back."

"How can you be so sure?"

"After I had finished with her, believe me, she will not be back."

"What did you do to her?"

"Nothing you need worry about. I just did what I was told to do. What I'm good at. End of story. Pass the pizza."

I got the message that she was now one topic that was off limit, so I stopped asking questions about her and moved on to my next, and ultimately more important, topic. Me. Or, more precisely, how long would it take before I turned into a vampire. I planned to ask my questions one at a time, sensibly, but there were so many piled up in my head they tumbled out one after another.

"How long before I have to go hunting and suck blood? How long before I grow wings? How long before I can smell and hear and run as fast as you can?"

"Slow down," the Rev stopped me as the words spewed out. "Slow down. Riley, have you been worried about this since last year?"

"Yes, of course I have. You told me that the only way to become a vampire was to drink the blood of one, and I did, in the theatre. I bit Severn and sucked his blood so he could fly. Of course I've been worrying about it ever since. How long does it take? What will happen to me?"

"Oh, Riley," the Rev sounded genuinely remorseful. "I wish you had spoken to me earlier. Severn why didn't you tell me she was so worried?"

"I didn't know either, until the other day, and I haven't had a chance to talk to you about it because of the Tommy drama."

The Rev sighed. "Riley, stop panicking. You are in no danger of changing. You didn't drink enough. The changeover has to be controlled. It's not a case of slurping a little of our blood and waiting. To start with, we have to drink enough of yours to leave your body needing to make more blood quickly. Then, before you can make more of your own, we replace it with ours. It takes quite a lot of our own, taken in several doses over a period of several days, to make our blood dominant over your natural human blood. Then, if we've got it right, all the changes you've asked about happen quite quickly. The hunger for blood starts immediately. The first thing you feel the need to do is feed. The senses, sight, hearing, intensify almost as fast because in order to feed you need to hunt and in order to hunt you need speed, stealth, hearing and sight. The wings come last. They start to grow within the first month but, let's face it, they're bloody big fully stretched, so they don't pop up overnight. They take about ten years, but it's fifteen to twenty years before they are big enough to fly with. Riley, you are human. You're going to stay human. You didn't drink enough of Severn's blood to make you anything else. The only way you can become one of us is if you choose to. You need to think about it. If you want to be one of us, we would welcome you aboard, but it needs to be your decision. It will not happen by accident and it will not happen without your full consent."

I sat, staring at him, speechless. Too much to take in. After months of asking those questions over and over in my head, after months of believing my whole world was about to change forever, I was normal. Normal. The same person I had always been. Not a vampire. Wow! I didn't know whether to laugh or cry.

Normal. I had a sudden realisation. For the last few months I had believed my whole world, my future, was changing and now it wasn't but for my best friend, Anita, her normal was never going to be the same again. She was going to be a mother. For the rest of her life. Her normal was about to change completely. The normal we had as school friends would change as well. Normal. What the hell was normal anyway? I snuggled up beside Severn thinking wild thoughts.

I gave Severn points for trying. He did his best to distract me from over-thinking but I had way too much swirling around in my head and he eventually gave up, content to sit on the couch and let me rest against him. Then it was back to Mona Vale to get ready for the evening show.

"Any word on Braden?" I asked Cameron as we past each other in the carpark.

"Yeah, I had a text. He's a lot better. Still a bit dizzy and pale but his Mum's stopped fussing over him so I think he'll live."

"Good, that's good."

"You staying for the party tonight?"

"Of course!"

"Good." Cameron looked genuinely pleased as he walked away, which made me feel pleased as well. Two admirers. One human boy-racer, one vampire. Decisions!

Like the afternoon show, the evening performance was an outstanding success. The excitement had grown to where the acting pace had picked up, so Severn and I were almost caught off guard a few times as songs and cues came faster than we expected. Down at ground level Aiden and the Rev had an easy time as equipment worked as it should and there were no earth loops, feedback problems or other disasters needing emergency repairs. In ten minutes less than it usually took the show was finished, the audience gone and it was party time.

An outdoor party on the lawn in front of the stage. With the promise of extra hands to help put it away later, Danny was convinced into leaving the lights and sound gear in place, and even happily played with the lighting desk to program in some fancy colour changes. Cameron came up with an mp3 player loaded with music which Severn connected to the sound desk and in a matter of minutes the stage became a dance floor. The ladies from the props department staggered from backstage under the weight of two trestle tables then seemingly out of nowhere plates of food appeared on them. The party got under way.

The biggest surprise was the arrival of the McCormacks. Angus looked relieved while Heidi was back to her old self – from the loud voice to the way-too-red lipstick and matching nail polish. Tommy basked in the fuss and was beginning to show off when he caught sight of me and froze. His eyes flicked sideways to Severn, languidly leaning on the scaffolding tower beside me, then back to me. His smile tightened and he quickly averted his gaze. Yep, he was definitely scared of us. Good. Now I was really sure that he would keep Severn's secret and never reveal the real transport he had to get down the hill.

In the end I wasn't sure if I enjoyed the party or not. Theoretically it was a great party – music, dancing, food, people having fun – but for me something just wasn't quite right. The whole vampire/not-vampire thing sat in my head, jumping forwards every time I relaxed. Severn noticed my distraction and suggested we take a walk and talk.

"What's wrong?" he asked as we negotiated the path around the edge of the lake. "Is it vampires in general, or me in particular?"

"Both, kind of, well, not you really, more me." I stumbled over my words, not able to get out what I needed to say.

We came across a park bench, so Severn pulled me down beside him and tried again.

"Start at the beginning and tell me what's bugging you."

"It's the whole vampire human thing. For the last few months I've thought I had no option, that I was becoming one of you so, even though I didn't know how it was going to work, I was getting my head around us being together for centuries, for ever. I was also getting my head around being, or at least looking like I was, sixteen years old for ever. It wasn't something I was happy about, but I didn't think I had any choice. It was too late. Now it isn't. The Rev says it's now my choice, and that's my problem. I don't know what to choose."

I paused for breath and to gauge Severn's reaction, which was unreadable. I continued.

"I think that we both think that, as girlfriend and boyfriend, we are doing okay and I hope it lasts for a long time. But, let's face it, we actually don't know each other that well. We've shared chocolate and coke backstage in a theatre, shared solving a murder and I've helped you kill someone. Now you're in a different country on the other side of the world and we only talk through the computer. What if it doesn't work? I mean, an ordinary … a non-vampire couple would go out, see how they got on then either stay together or move on. But, and here's the big but, if we're going to be together, then it really is going to be for ever, like ever and ever and ever, so we have to be really, really sure that it's going to work. Because the other part of being together is that I am going to have to become a vampire. You can't change back to being a human to be with me, so I'm going to have to change into a vampire, give up everything and everyone, to be with you. So I have to be sure it's going to work. I have to know!"

Severn nodded his understanding and I ploughed onto my last point.

"And the age thing. Doesn't it piss you guys off that you look like teenagers, for ever?"

"Yes," Severn acknowledged.

"Don't you wish you'd been older when you were changed?"

"Yes."

"Well, likewise. There is no way I want to be stuck at sixteen for the next several hundred years. Twenties would be okay, but then again, you look no more than eighteen, so I would have to make a decision soon."

"Why can't we just stay the way we are?" Severn asked. "I think it's amazing that you know what I am and you're still here. You could always come to France with me without having to change over. Wouldn't that be enough?"

I shook my head. "For now, maybe, but I'm going to age and you're not. Sixteen to eighteen works but one day I'll be sixty and you'll still look eighteen. That is so not going to work."

"So what do you think we should do?"

I took both his hands in mine and looked squarely into his eyes.

"Right now I think we should enjoy ourselves. If I've learned one thing from this whole Tommy business is that normal is not permanent. What's normal today might be completely different tomorrow and my mission now is to get my head around what my normal actually is. I have a vampire boyfriend, a pregnant best friend and a new sister in Australia who I really should go and meet. I'm going to take these things one at a time. My vampire boyfriend is only here for another week, then he'll be off in his Lear jet back to his monastery, so I'm going to spend this week enjoying his company, in every way possible."

I let the full meaning of my words sink in and watched a small grin appear on Severn's face as he realised what I meant. I grinned back then carried on.

"Then, when he's gone I'm going to drown my sorrows by getting on a plane to Australia to visit my sister. I might even ask if I can bring my best friend along as well and we can go shopping in the biggest shopping mall I can find. Then school will start again and I will work my backside off to finish my final year with good marks. Then, and only then, will I think seriously about whether or not I want to become a vampire."

"Fair enough," Severn smiled a broad smile and squeezed my hands in obvious relief. "I think that's fair enough. I get it, I do. Actually, I'm relieved. When I was changed, if a month or so later I had been told I was still human I would have run a mile. There is no way I would have had anything to do with vampires ever again. As soon as I heard the Rev tell you that you weren't changing I thought it was all over for us. All evening I've been expecting you to tell me that we were over. I can't believe you still want me around. I love the bit about us getting closer and I'm going to keep convincing you that we need to be together by offering you tempting bribes like Lear jet trips to Australia, or France, whenever you get sick of the weather here." He laughed. "I've got to stay ahead of that damned lighting boy with the fancy car somehow."

CHAPTER THIRTY ONE

I slept in. We were the last to leave the party because we had to pack up all the equipment. In spite of the promises, hardly anybody had stayed to help and it was nearly four in the morning before I made it into bed. By myself. Regardless of what I had suggested to Severn, I was exhausted and he was hungry so, with a quick kiss, we parted company at the front door. Mum let me sleep as long as possible but as there was a Sunday matinee to do, she woke me up with an offer of lunch. I was going to refuse and grab another hour's sleep till she told me that Severn was already waiting for me in the kitchen.

I was out of bed, dressed and in the kitchen in record time only to find Mum waving a five dollar note at me instead of the coffee I was hoping for.

"Milk," she said. "We need milk. Can you two pop down to the dairy and grab some please?"

There was no point arguing as that would only delay the much-needed caffeine fix so I grabbed Severn's hand, pulled him out of the chair and out the door. I felt like a normal girlfriend as we walked, hand in hand, around the corner and down the road to the corner dairy. We talked about normal things like the flowers in the neighbour's garden and what type of dog her funny little barking monster actually was. The weather was fine, the sky cloudless. All beautifully normal. Until we reached the dairy and learned what Aiden had done.

We stared, transfixed with horror as we read the banner headline in the morning paper.

'Woman's body found on New Brighton beach'

Severn gasped.

"Not again! I don't believe it!"

Other Books by J.L. O'Rourke

Blood in the Wings

The First of Severn.

Vampires and murder backstage in a Christchurch theatre. 16 year old Riley Lowe is working as a stage hand, backstage at her theatre company's annual show. Her classmate from school, Tasha, is also in the show as a dancer and, as usual, she is flirting with all the guys. In particular, she is trying to take the one Riley is attracted to. Severn is one of a group of professional theatre crew who are helping with the show but the closer she gets to him, the more Riley realises that there is something strange about the group who live and work in the dark. When Tasha is killed and Severn disappears, Riley learns their terrible secret. But can she solve the murder in time to save Severn?

Read an excerpt:

The rain came down red and Severn was gone.

The police asked me lots of questions, both at the theatre and, later, down at the police station but I couldn't tell them much more than that. No, that's not true. I could have told them heaps more, but I didn't. Anyway, I wasn't sure myself. No, don't tell anyone anything. Just answer their questions, get out of here, find Severn and hope the answers are wrong.

"Tell me again, Miss Lowe, take it slowly." The policeman, a detective inspector I think he said he was, kept tapping his pen against the table. It was driving me crazy. The policewoman sitting by the door smiled. That was driving me crazy too.

"What do you know about this Severn?"

I have to think about the answer. I know things about Severn that nobody knows but I hardly know him at all. And I desperately want to keep on learning.

So, really slowly like the cop wants, I start from the beginning again.

"I met Severn two weeks ago when we packed in." It feels like forever.

"Packed in?" the cop inquires.

"Yeah, that's what I said. Pack-in. It's theatre-speak, Get used to it!" This guy was so dumb.

"All right, Miss Lowe," the cop snapped. "There's no need to get abusive. Let's just get on with it so we can all go home."

"Yeah, well don't butt in then!" Okay, it was well after midnight and I was tired and cranky, but he really was a jerk. "I told you, I met him at pack-in. That's when we set up the show in the theatre." I added the last bit slowly, just in case he was as stupid as he looked in his prissy black jacket and his ugly blue tie,

Then, as he still looked blank, I explained.

"Until pack-in the show is all over the place. The actors will have been rehearsing in one place, the orchestra somewhere else and the dancers somewhere else again. The props and the wardrobe have been made at the main rehearsal rooms over the last few months and the sets have been made in a hired warehouse. At least that's how our company usually works."

The cop was rapidly taking notes.

"On pack-in day the set and all the technical stuff such as the lights and the sound gear arrives at the theatre and the crew take over; rigging, wiring, hauling things into place. It's organised chaos. I love it."

"Why were you there?"

"Mum's been in the society for years. Even before she went to Australia and met Dad. When they split up she came home and joined up again. I go with her."

"You act?"

"No, I'm the family disappointment. Backstage, that's my job. I'm doing theatre arts at school but only because it's easy, not because I ever want to act!"

He was actually writing this down, he really was a jerk!

"But you were at this show?" he asked, looking up from his paper.

"Yeah, I just told you, I work backstage. My theatre arts teacher also happened to be the choreographer for this year's show and she talked to the stage manager who agreed I could work as floor crew, moving bits of set on and off stage when the scenes change.

This year's production is the biggest show we've done. The

director decided to have all the scene changes happening with the curtains up but in a black-out and there're about twenty-one scene changes so they needed a lot of crew. That's how come Severn and his lot were there at all. We didn't have enough people to move all the sets by ourselves, or do the complicated lighting the show needs, so the stage manager rang somebody who rang somebody else who suggested Seth Borman.

"Seth Borman," the cop repeated as he wrote the name on his piece of paper.

"That's what I said."

The cop glared at me.

"It was a good idea," I continued. "Even if it is costing the society an arm and a leg. He runs a professional travelling stage crew. Technical wizards."

"And Severn was one of these?" the cop asked.

"Yeah," I snapped back. "I was just getting to that." I carried on.

"Seth Borman's the leader. The head flyman." I could see the cop's eyebrow start to rise with a question so I jumped in first. "Flymen are the guys who work on a little platform about fifteen metres above the stage, hauling the big backdrop cloths and bits of set in and out. They are immensely strong. Seth Borman has an upper body to die for," I added wistfully.

The cop glared at me again. I continued.

"There are six more of them. The women, Olivia and Meredith, work floor crew like I do. So does Aiden, Meredith's twin brother. The older guy, Finn, is the floor electrician. The guy in charge of lighting is a strange little dude they call the Reverend. He's about five foot nothing tall and wears a huge black floor-length coat that makes him look like a miniature version of Darth Vader. I've never seen him without a can of coke in one hand and a chocolate bar in the other.

Severn operates the sound board.

I didn't notice him for the first four days.

Tasha saw him first. When it comes to men, she always does. She's got some sort of inbuilt radar detector that homes in on good-looking men. Mind you, it must be a sending as well as receiving device because they home in on her just as fast.

Tasha was in the show as a dancer. She clicked around backstage in tap shoes and a scarlet bathing costume covered in ostrich feathers, all up in front and out behind. I hate Tasha, she's such a bitch."

"Tasha? Would that be Natasha Moreland?" The cop looked up at me. I nodded. "You said you hate Natasha?" he inquired, tapping his pen again. "Why is that?"

"No, no," I backtracked fast. "I don't hate her really, I just said that, you know, like you do, I don't mean it. She's my friend, actually. She's just, you know, so pretty and everything, And she knows it. She knew it that night, that's for sure."

It was during interval at the final dress rehearsal. We had gone out into the alleyway at the stage door to get some fresh air. It was even darker outside than it had been backstage. We were standing by the open stage door where there was still a bit of light, watching Aiden and Finn playing hackey. I barely noticed Severn and the Reverend leaning against the fire escape off to one side, sharing a can of coke. Until Tasha nodded her head in their direction.

"They're a weird unit, those two."

"You reckon?" I replied automatically as I stole a glance in their direction. They made an interesting study.

Severn, the taller and probably the elder, stood shyly, shoulders hunched and arms folded protectively across his chest. He had one leg folded over the other so he kind of resembled a nesting stork. In complete contrast was the Reverend. Younger, smaller but full of confidence. He stood firmly, his head back, his shortish brown pony tail bobbing against the collar of his oversize coat as he punctuated a sentence with much waving of the coke can.

"Nicely put together though," I finally answered.

"Hmmm," Tasha snorted. "More your type."

Tasha always says that when she means she doesn't fancy a guy herself. Mind you, she's often right. She was this time. Tasha is into bodies. Big work-out-at-the-gym-every-night type bodies. She was already torn between Seth Borman and the leading man who was the only other import into the company. He'd been brought in from Auckland especially to play the lead as none of our men came up to scratch. A move that was causing ripples of discontent.

I looked again at Severn's long, slender body packed so nicely into his black jeans and long-sleeved black T-shirt with the show's logo and the word "crew" in red so it won't show up on stage, and agreed. Kind of cute.

"Definitely."

"So let's do it." Tasha was into direct action. She pushed herself away from the wall which had been propping her up, flicked her scarlet ostrich plumes and clicked her way across the alley. I followed bemused.

"Spare any of that coke for a gasping dancer?" She broke into their conversation, whipping the can from the Reverend's hand before he could reply. She took a drink and handed it to me before turning back to them. "I'm Tasha, this is Riley. You can talk to us, we don't bite."

The Reverend tilted his head back and managed to look down at her from below. He gave a maliciously sweet smile. "We do." With a wicked giggle he plucked the can from my hand, drained it, crushed it and tossed it into the nearby rubbish bin. "They call me the Reverend. This is Severn."

"Why?" Tasha sounded confused.

"Because he is."

"Not him. You. Why the Reverend?"

"Because I am."

Beside him Severn sniggered. I looked up at him and he flashed me a smile. Without speaking he reached over and felt in one of the Reverend's voluminous pockets, pulled out another can of coke, broke it open and passed it to me.

"You're floor crew, right?" he finally spoke, his voice a light tenor that matched his laugh.

"Yeah. Why Seven?" If Tasha didn't want to know, I did. "Is it because there's seven of you?"

"No. Not the number seven. With an R, like the English river."

"Oh, right." I felt stupid. I also felt the all-too-embarrassing heat of a blush creeping up my neck and into my face. I gave a quick prayer of thanks that it was dark in the alley. Cover it up. "What are you? Follow spot or something? You're not on the floor, I would have seen you."

"Nah," he shook his head with a slight grin. I was sure he had seen my face go red. "I've passed you lots of times. You're right, I'm not floor crew, I'm sound, but I've been backstage every night with the radio mics." He laughed self-depreciatingly. "I didn't think you'd noticed."

Now I felt guilty, like I'd snubbed him on purpose but I was saved from having to reply by a call from the stage door.

"Act two beginners on stage!"

I took another quick gulp from the can before handing it back as we headed back into the backstage gloom.

Power Ride

An Avi Livingstone Murder Mystery

Kester (Kit) Simmons, drummer with the rock band 'Charlotte Jane', was out of beat. He was stressed out, starving and he thought he was going crazy. Then, with less than two weeks to go before a national tour, Kit's precious drums and one of the band members are found slashed to pieces. The keyboard player, Avi Livingstone, is missing, Kit has no alibi and, to make matters worse, the police suspect him of dealing drugs.

Read an excerpt:

The weary-looking blond was not amused.

"Stop!" His shouted command cut through the sound pumping from the Marshall amplifiers, stopping his five fellow musicians in mid bar.

"Hold it!" The blond spun round to face the drummer.

"Kit, it's no bloody good, man. It's not bloody working. And it's not bloody good enough. What's with you, man? This is old hat! We've done it a million times, a dozen already today. You're always telling me you can do this number in your sleep; so sleep then, because today you sure as hell can't do it when you're awake!"

The man half-hidden behind the rack of shining black Tama drums moved both his sticks to his right hand, freeing his left to push a lock of long, sweat-dampened black hair back into place.

"I'm sorry," he said softly. "It's just... I'm a bit... um... I'm just not very together."

"We noticed."

"Look, can we take a break? I don't feel so good."

The blond shrugged and, as an answer, unstrapped his ageing Gibson guitar and propped it up onto a conveniently placed support stand.

"Why not? It certainly can't make this damned rehearsal go

any worse."

Kester Simmons pushed the unruly lock of hair back into place again then unthreaded his long, lean body from behind his drums.

"I really am sorry, Danny," he sighed.

The blond replied with a savage glare.

"I don't want apologies, Kit, I want a drum beat. Damn it all, Kit, it just isn't good enough. We are hitting the road on tour in just over a week - ten days to be precise - and this rehearsal has been a complete bloody disaster!" Daniel Gordon was working himself into a mild frenzy.

Kester turned to walk away but Danny had wound himself up and continued his harangue.

"And another thing, Mr Simmons! If your 'not feeling too good' means what it usually does, you'd better get your act together and you had better do it damned fast. It's a long tour and we're not babysitting you through it this time. You had better be on deck all the bloody way!" His voice dropped to a malicious hiss. "Don't you forget for one minute, Kit, that we are running real close to not making this tour at all, and it's all your fault."

"Hey, come on now!"

"That's below the belt!" The keyboard player and the rhythm guitarist leapt simultaneously to Kit's defence.

"That was below the belt and decidedly uncalled for," the rhythm guitarist, Mike Kiesanowski, repeated himself. "We are slightly behind schedule because our bass player quit. That was not Kit's fault and we are getting mighty sick of you hassling him about it."

"Huh!" Danny snorted in fury and stormed off towards the coffee-making facilities at the other end of the old converted carpenter's workshop the band used as a permanent rehearsal venue.

Without acknowledging Mike's spirited defence of him, Kit dropped his drumsticks into his gear bag and headed out the door into the garden which formed the surroundings for both the rehearsal room and Kit's own quaint little settler's cottage. Once outside he leaned his back against the wall, took a couple of deep breaths, ran both hands through his hair in a sign of despair then began a methodical but unsuccessful search of his pockets for a packet of cigarettes. Finding none, he muttered an unintelligible curse and slid down the wall into a sitting position. A few seconds later another figure flung itself down beside him and placed an arm around Kit's shoulders.

"You okay?"

Kit looked at the concerned expression behind the gold-rimmed glasses that framed the keyboard player's face and gave a wan smile.

"I'm not great, but I'll live." His smile opened into the hopeful, innocent expression normally seen on spaniel pups. "Hey, you wouldn't have a spare cigarette by any chance?"

Avi Livingstone pulled a squashed packet of Rothmans from the hip pocket of his ancient, faded Levis. He flicked it open but it revealed only the tattered remains of a cigarette which Avi threw away.

"Sorry, Kit, that's it. How come you're scavenging again anyway? Can't you afford your own?"

"Um... no," Kit replied apologetically. "I'm broke."

Avi sat back and his soulful brown eyes subjected Kit to a long, searching appraisal.

"Look, Kit," he said eventually, "I know it's none of my business but was Danny's comment on the mark? I mean, you're broke already, and it's still early in the week, you say you're not feeling very well and, let's face it, your drumming's been half a beat off all morning."

Avi let the comment hang in the air but Kit declined to answer, content to scuff the ground in front of him with the toe of his boot. Avi patted Kit gently on the shoulder.

"Come on, Kit, this is Avi. An honest answer, okay?"

Kit rounded on him, flicked Avi's hand away and snapped a reply.

"An honest answer? Oh yeah? And you're all going to believe me, just like that? I know what you all think. It doesn't matter what I say, you'll all believe whatever you damned well want to. And I suppose you'll be checking up on me with Gabriel behind my back."

"Hey, come on, calm down." Avi gently restrained Kit from getting up and leaving. "Calm down. I repeat, this is Avi you're talking to, not Danny, not Gabriel. I believe you. I always believe you. When have I ever not believed you? Come on, now, talk to me, what's wrong?"

"Sorry." Kit slumped back against the wall. "Honest answer? I'm broke because my money's been cut back again and I can't manage, not that I ever could. Mum and Gabriel said I got behind on the power and phone bills, even though I was sure that I'd been keeping up, so they've taken power of attorney over my money again. Gabriel pays everything for me and gives me a pathetically small amount of pocket money, which leads me back to my original statement - I'm broke!"

"Power of attorney? Can they do that at your age?"

"Oh yeah, you'd better believe they can! All my money is handled by them through a trust anyway, since I was in hospital last time, so I can't do anything about it - except grovel desperately."

"And you've been a naughty boy and spent your allowance already," Avi teased.

"Don't rub it in, it's humiliating enough."

"Sorry"

"Yeah, so I've got no cigarettes and Mum's out of town today so I couldn't phone her and hit her up for a loan - not that she'd give me money for cigarettes anyway. I'd just get yet another moralising lecture on the virtues of quitting. In answer to your other accusations, I know I'm drumming like an epileptic praying mantis but I'm not feeling very well and I don't feel well because I'm pretty stressed out. But it's just that, Avi, stress. I am not - repeat not - underlined, in capital letters not - stoned. Okay? Get that? Not stoned! Out of all of them, Avi, you should know I've been clean for over a year. You guys are as bad as Mum and Gabriel. They don't trust me either."

"Of course I trust you. I was just worried. Hey, if you're stressed out it's because something's bothering you. Can I help in any way? I'm here any time you need me, you know that. Do you want to talk about it?"

"Thanks, but no thanks. I'll be okay. I just need a cigarette."

Eighteen years of friendship had taught Avi when not to push Kit, so he backed off, lightening the tone.

"Tell you what then, why don't we leave Danny to cool off and sneak down to the dairy. I'll buy us a packet of cigarettes and we can share them."

"Um... I don't know when I can pay you back."

"So, who's counting? Leave it to me in your will," Avi grinned as he hauled Kit's lanky body to its feet. "Come on, before the pocket battleship launches another offensive."

By the time the two men had returned to the workshop Daniel Gordon had left. The band's replacement bass player, Kelly Reynolds, their temporary backing vocalist, Joanna Greenwood, and Mike Kiesanowski were ensconced comfortably in three of the dilapidated arm chairs which formed a casual semi-circle around the primitive coffee-making facilities at the far end of the large room. Avi and Kit slumped into two of the other chairs, Kit completing the act by stretching his long legs out to rest silver decorated, black leather boots on the badly stained coffee table. Joanna lifted her tiny trainer-clad foot and kicked Kit's off the table.

"Get your feet off the table, you lanky slob!"

"It's my table," Kit argued petulantly, although he obliged, but only because Joanna had pushed his feet off and he couldn't find the energy to put them back on.

"So where's our beloved leader?" asked Avi, craning his neck to scan the room.

"He gave up on you lot, called you by all sorts of interesting descriptive phrases - especially you, Kit, then ordered a lunch break," Mike replied. "We have two hours of carefree liberty after which he expects us to perform - or else!"

"That wasn't how he phrased it," Joanna smiled.

"No, that's the edited version fit for human consumption."

"Great," said Avi. "So why are you lot still hanging around here?"

"We were awaiting your return to ascertain whether or not you wished to accompany us to luncheon."

Avi grinned at the young man who had given the pompous-sounding reply. Kelly Reynolds was a recent arrival to the group and was still somewhat of an enigma. Mike, Avi and Kit were founding members of the group, 'Charlotte Jane', and were old friends from way back. Mike had met Avi and Kit when the band was first formed; Avi and Kit went back even further, to their first days at Beckenham Primary School eighteen years before. Joanna, although new to the group, was a long-standing acquaintance. She was Avi's cousin and in the tight-knit world of their parent's religious community the two had grown up closely together. Danny Gordon wasn't a local by birth, but he had been around long enough to be considered part of the Christchurch musical establishment. He came originally from Geraldine, a small rural community south of Christchurch, but generally chose not to broadcast that fact too widely. Daniel Gordon had a serious self-image problem.

Kelly Reynolds, on the other hand, seemed eminently self-assured. He had a different style to the others. His short, trendy haircut and snappy fashion clothing contrasted markedly with the more traditional 'long-haired scruffy rock musician' image of Kit and Avi, and his way of speaking matched his style. It wasn't as if he was being consciously pompous either. Kelly came from an upper-crust Wellington family and had all the benefits of an expensive private school education. The accent came naturally, along with an eclectic knowledge of world affairs, an innate sense of style and, as Joanna had often noted, an elegant, almost balletic, way of moving. To Joanna's eyes, at least, Kelly was a very tasty package.

Kelly acknowledged Avi's grin at his accent with a slight bow of his head. He grinned back and continued, "Then the telephone rang for Kester."

Kit looked up, flicking the hair out of his eyes with a gesture that was so habitual it had been become almost subconscious.

"Who was it?" he asked.

"I'm afraid I don't know," Kelly shrugged. "He didn't say. He merely inquired if Kester Simmons, and he did use Kester, not Kit, was there. I said you had disappeared temporarily with Avrahim and that we had placed bets on the probable destination being the corner dairy. Fair guess? Anyway, I inquired if I could take a message but he declined and hung up. I'm afraid he failed to leave a name or a contact number."

He shrugged his shoulders expressively and stared at Kit whose face now registered a broad grin.

"Yes!" Kit shouted, punching the air with a fist. "Awesome!"

Joanna turned to Avi. "That makes sense to you, does it?"

Avi grinned and shook his head.

"No, but that's normal with Kit, he never makes any sense."

"Well, I have no intentions of playing guessing games, especially when I haven't been fed. To hell with you guys, I'm going to find some lunch. There is no way I am going to put up with any more of Daniel Gordon's little hissy fits on an empty stomach." So saying, Jo pulled an orange nylon parka from the back of the chair in which Kelly was languidly sprawled, thrust her arms into the jacket's sleeves and headed purposely towards the door.

"You know something?" Kelly said to no-one in particular, "The lovely lady has made an infinitely practical suggestion. Shall we join her?"

There was a general mumbling of agreement as the men rose to their feet and trooped out to follow Jo. As the party wended its way around Oxford Terrace, Joanna dropped back to fall into step with Avi.

"Cousin, tell me something. Kit's a bit out of it, isn't he? Do tours always have this effect on him?"

"Tours? No, they don't affect him at all, strangely enough," Avi replied thoughtfully. "Something is obviously bugging him, though. Mind you, that doesn't mean to say that it'll be anything horrendous. Kit doesn't have the most stable personality and he is apt to make monstrous mountains out of the most minute of molehills. Whatever it is, he doesn't want to talk about it. This, with Kit, means that it is probably something reasonably serious, but I can't force him to talk to me. I'll have another go later. I can usually convince him to talk, it's just a matter of easing him along gently. I can be very persuasive." He ignored Jo's expression of sarcasm. "I wouldn't worry about it too much, though. In the meantime, I would think the best thing we can do is keep Danny from ripping Kit's face off this afternoon."

"Danny doesn't like Kit much, does he?"

"Huh!" Avi's laugh was more a scoff of derision. "Rest assured, cousin dearest, it's nothing personal. This close to a tour, Danny hates everyone, including and especially himself. Tours might not affect Kit, but they blow Danny away. He'll get worse yet."

"Super." Jo did not sound as if she actually meant the superlative. "You mean we're likely to see some fireworks?"

"Better than Old Man Carson's bonfires. I guarantee it."

Joanna laughed and rubbed her hands gleefully. Then she stopped and looked serious.

"But Danny's such a little guy. He wouldn't be stupid enough to upset the whole band would he? Surely?"

"He would, he has and he will, no doubt, do so again. In case you hadn't noticed, Daniel Gordon is somewhat akin to your neighbour's crazed Jack Russell terrier. Wind him up enough and he'll tackle anything, even if it is three times his size. Mind you, we could have some real problems this tour. I don't think it's going to be a very smooth ride. Danny is still very angry about losing our last bass player and, even though we've got Kelly, Danny is determined to hold Kit responsible and to rub it in as much as possible."

"Why?"

Avi shrugged his shoulders and spread his hands wide in a gesture of genuine incomprehension.

"I don't know. Danny's just a creep, I guess."

"So why keep him in the band, if he's such a creep?"

"Two reasons, I guess. He's a damn good guitarist and vocalist and he sells records."

"Garbage! The band sells records, not Danny Gordon. 'Charlotte Jane' was selling records before Danny joined you guys, and who the hell was he? Some two-bit wanna-be from Geraldine! Come on, Avi, he might be a good guitarist but they're ten a penny. If the man is a jerk you've got to have a better reason than that for keeping him on."

Avi ran his hand thoughtfully over his unshaven chin. He shrugged again.

"You know something, Jo? I don't have a decent answer. I guess we've got so used to Danny being a prize prick we just take his temper tantrums for granted. I mean, nobody's perfect, and if we started throwing out band members who had personality problems there'd be bugger all of us left. Poor old Kit would be at the top of the list, he's completely scrambled, and I don't think I'm always the easiest musician to work with. Anyway, whatever Danny is, he's a good businessman. He's got a pretty watertight contract, so we're stuck with him for the duration, at least."

"The duration of what?"

"The cd, the tour and the next single. It could be an exhausting few months."

About the Author

J. L. O'Rourke has worked as a journalist, sub-editor, free-lance writer and office administrator. When not writing, she enjoys being in a theatre, either onstage as a singer or backstage where she has been everything from floor crew to stage-manager. She lives in Christchurch, New Zealand, with an assortment of hairless dogs, fluffy cats and grumpy guinea pigs.

You can email her at

mailto:editor@millwheelpress.co.nz

or follow her on Facebook at

https://www.facebook.com/MillwheelPress

www.ingramcontent.com/pod-product-compliance
Lightning Source LLC
Chambersburg PA
CBHW071309130626
46556CB00004B/1536